I saw the lemon pale sunlight that streaked the bare dark floor but left the rest of the big room in shadow. I heard the tap-tap of Jeremy's mallet as he worked on the sculpture of my head, and through it, the shallow whisper of my own labored breath.

Jeremy, leaning over the table, was saying softly, "You're beautiful, Teena. So very beautiful. Your hair is golden and glowing . . . "

I fought the hypnotic rhythm of his words as once again, I allowed my fingers to creep back to the tender spot where he had left his kiss, that faintly-remembered kiss, through which I had at last learned the unbelievable truth about him and the curse that he bore. . . .

Books by Daoma Winston

Vampire Curse
Dennison Hill

Published by
WARNER PAPERBACK LIBRARY

THE VAMPIRE CURSE

Daoma Winston

WARNER
PAPERBACK
LIBRARY

A Warner Communications Company

FOR CINDY AND KEN MORRIS,
and GARY MORRIS
Taos Inn, Taos, New Mexico

WARNER PAPERBACK LIBRARY EDITION
First Printing: January, 1971
Second Printing: March, 1975

Cover illustration by Ben Wohlberg

Warner Paperback Library is a division of Warner Books, Inc.,
75 Rockefeller Plaza, New York, N.Y. 10019.

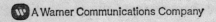 A Warner Communications Company

Printed in the United States of America

CHAPTER ONE

Suddenly I saw the pale lemon sunlight that streaked the bare dark floor but left the rest of the big room in shadow.

I heard the humming silence that surrounded me, and through it, the slow shallow whisper of my own laboring breath.

I vaguely remembered a sensation of having been somehow outside of myself, a distant observer seeing my awareness as a tiny candle flame that rose and fell, danced and flickered, shrank and grew large. And then I was awake without knowing for certain that I had actually been asleep.

I was awake, yes, but drifting still. I was weary and weak, but I clung to faint recollections that melted away like wind-driven mist as I tried to seize and examine them.

Jeremy had been leaning over the table, his low voice speaking softly. "You're beautiful, Teena. So very beautiful. I knew the moment that you came out of the storm, the moment I saw you, what you must become to me. Your hair is golden and glowing, the way it was in that terrible rainy day, as if it were the only spot in the world touched by sunlight. Your brown eyes, so wide and eager, and somehow sad. The lift of your chin. Your sudden smile, Teena. Oh, yes, yes, so beautiful, and now, now, too, Teena . . ." Jeremy's low murmuring voice, going on and on.

There had been the tap of the mallet as he worked on the sculpture of my face that he had finally, after much persuasion, made me promise to sit for every day.

His voice . . .

The sound of the mallet . . .

The sunlight paling . . .

The shadows reaching . . .

His footsteps approaching . . .

His lips at my throat . . .

And now I fought the terrible tiredness. I saw the pale lemon sun on the bare dark floor.

I straightened in my chair. My fingers moved, trembled at the place where he had left his kiss.

5

"Oh, Teena, love. You've moved and ruined the pose," he chided me. "How do you imagine I can work, if you won't ever sit still?"

But, listening hard, I heard that his deep voice was full of satisfaction, of hunger assuaged and appeased. He straightened, dropped the mallet on the table, and flexed his long hands. The pale sun touched his lean face, brightened glittering embers in his dark eyes. A sardonic smile curled his thin, blood-red lips. "Or perhaps you really don't want me to," he went on, the familiar lulling sound slowing his words to a terrifying and hypnotic rhythm. "Perhaps it just doesn't mean anything to you that with every stroke I make in this marble I am expressing my love for you."

I fought the hypnotic rhythm of his words. I struggled to keep myself from wildly agreeing that yes, yes, he was right. I did want him to sculpt my face, that I would do willingly without his love. Once again I allowed my fingers to creep back to the tender spot where he had left his kiss, that faintly remembered kiss, through which I had at last learned the unbelievable truth.

It was a truth that seemed like madness. So much like madness that I dared not scream my accusation aloud.

Who would credit it?

Who would help me?

Those terrifying suspicions which I had tried for weeks to suppress were now confirmed. I no longer dared doubt my certainty. For that way surely lay the path of despair and death.

Jeremy was asking, "Teena, love, what is it?"

I told myself quickly that he mustn't know that I had guessed what he was.

I summoned what meager strength I could and managed to smile at him. "I'm sorry, Jeremy. I'm just so tired. Would you mind if we stop for today?"

"You're always so tired lately," he complained.

Secret laughter glinted in his eyes. I wondered if he was mocking me. But he was right. For three weeks now, ever since he had begun to work my face with chisel and mallet into white marble, I had felt my strength waning,

6

my flesh melting, my bones softening. For three weeks I had sensed my courage failing, and hope dying.

Now I knew why.

Jeremy sighed deeply. "All right. If that's what you want, then we can stop for today."

I rose slowly, carefully. My body felt limp and boneless within the white dress he insisted that I wear for posing. My knees trembled. My pulse pounded from weakness or from fear. I didn't know.

"Poor Teena, you *are* tired out, aren't you?" he said. He crossed the room. His lean hard arm encircled my waist. "I'll help you to your room."

"I'm all right," I said quickly, shrinking within the imprisonment of his arm, swept with revulsion at his touch.

He sensed the intensity of my withdrawal. He gave me what I was sure then was a mocking look. "Why, Teena, love, how can you still be so shy with me? After all, we *are* engaged. It was love at first sight, wasn't it? And for both of us? So you mustn't act as if I'm a monster when I touch you." He went on, sudden laughter in his voice. "Surely you don't think I'm a monster, Teena."

I made myself smile again. I pretended that I didn't understand the double meaning in his lightly spoken words, that I didn't recognize the arrogance that made those words possible. I pretended that I didn't remember drifting in hypnotic sleep while he bent over me, his lips at my throat, draining strength and sustenance and life from my body as he must have done to May and Sarah and all the others. I promised myself that I would not be his victim too.

He was a monster, yes. But more, much more.

I wouldn't allow myself to give the name to what he really was.

As he led me down the long dim hall to my room, still holding me within the imprisoning circle of his arms, I wondered how I would face the ordeal that lay ahead of me, how I would find the wit to save myself. . . .

The nightmare began nearly four thousand miles away from the great stone house called Rentlow Retreat that perched on a cliff high above the rocky New England coast.

I sat on a terrace, warmed by golden Mediterranean sun, watching the pale shadows of the silver olive trees dance across Margaretha's face.

She put the tiny expresso cup on the mosaic table, glanced at me through her huge black sunglasses, and said casually, "I think you'd better begin to plan your packing, Teena. You'll only have four days, and it will probably take you all that time just to decide what you will want to take with you."

"Take with me?" I echoed blankly. "But where are we going?"

"Not we, Teena. You."

"Me? Alone? Where? Why?" I was too bewildered to hide the quick panic that swept me.

But Margaretha ignored the clear tremor that shook my voice and acknowledged only the bewilderment. She sighed. "Oh, Teena, really. You must have guessed. After all, you're eighteen years old. And you do have eyes in your head, even if you don't always want to use them."

The golden sun was suddenly less warm. The pale shadows cast by the olive trees seemed to darken. I was beginning to understand, but I didn't want to. I was afraid to. I said, "I don't know what you're talking about."

"I'm talking about me, and Timothy Bye. Surely you realized that we are quite serious about each other, that we would decide to marry."

"But, Mother . . ." I protested, and stopped quickly, knowing that to call her Mother would only annoy her. "But, Margaretha . . ." I began again, while she frowned at me, " . . . even if you do marry Timothy . . ."

Her frown deepened. "Not if, Teena. I shall. And as soon as we do, we're leaving the Riviera, closing up the villa for good. We'll be taking a six-month honeymoon in South America, combining it with an archaeological dig Timothy has planned for a long time. So . . ."

"Couldn't I go with you?" I begged.

"Teena, really! What would Timothy think if I were to suggest taking my eighteen-year-old daughter along on our honeymoon?" She laughed softly. "Besides, it's time that you detached yourself from my apron strings. You're entirely too timid. Why, you're very nearly backward, you're so immature for your age." She sighed. "I suppose it's my fault. I've let you be overprotected and spoiled. But now, as I told you, you must face growing up."

"What do you want me to do?" I whispered. "Where do you plan for me to go?"

She passed a slender hand over her dark curly hair, and stretched her long beautiful legs. She took off her dark glasses so that I could see the hot glow of her blue eyes.

She was thirty-eight years old, I knew, but she looked much younger, and as lovely now as she must have been before I was born.

The girls at the Swiss boarding school from which I had graduated just a few months before had always envied me on her rare visits to see me. They said she was as beautiful as a movie star. They didn't understand that I had learned to fear her beauty. It drew men to her. It led her to search for new hearts to conquer. The search meant change. And I feared change as much as I feared her beauty.

There had already been too many dislocations in my life.

First there had been Ben, my father, Ben Halliday. I hadn't seen him for twelve years, not since Margaretha divorced him and left the United States to live in our villa on the Italian Riviera, and then to marry Arthur Haines. I hadn't seen Ben, nor heard from him, since the day he hugged me close, whispered, "Be a good girl, Teena baby, and remember that I love you."

But I'd never forgotten him. I knew what he looked like, and how his arms felt around me, and I was certain that someday I would find him again.

Arthur Haines had been good to me, kind in his casual way, occasionally interested, but when Margaretha and he divorced four years earlier, I hardly missed him.

And now there would be Timothy, and everything would be changed. I would leave the villa, leave Maria, who had taken care of me since I was six years old, leave Tony, who had always allowed me to play in the gardens he tended.

"It's all arranged," Margaretha said. "I wrote to my

sister, your Aunt June. I expect that you might just remember her." She ignored my negative headshake and went on. "June, and her husband, your Uncle Charles, will be delighted to have you. And it'll be wonderful for you, Teena. Your cousin Estrella is just a year older than you, and your cousin Jeremy is twenty-four. You'll have a great deal in common with those two, I'm sure."

"But they're strangers to me, Margaretha."

"They are your family," she said coolly. "And it's time that you knew them. And it's time, too, that you knew your own country."

I knew that it was no use to remind her that it was she who had taken me away from my own country, taken me away from my closeness with my family.

I said, "Just the same, I don't know anything about them."

Margaretha grinned suddenly, fluffed her hair. "There really isn't all that much to know. Charles is pleasant, but dull. Unless he's changed. Which I doubt. Poor Charles, he was once madly in love with me. But he made the mistake of introducing me to Ben. Yes, that's how I met your father actually. It was through Charles. They're related somehow. Third or fourth cousins, perhaps. Anyway, I married Ben, and Charles decided to settle for June. Oh, he was surprised when he discovered that neither June nor I had any money. Charles dragged June back to Rentlow Retreat, and there they've been ever since. That's one thing I'll say for Ben. He wasn't a fortune hunter. He was more than willing to accept me as I was. But I . . . well, that's a different story." She fluffed her hair again, and a huge diamond sparkled at me. I knew that Timothy must have given it to her, and she was expecting me to exclaim over it.

But I folded my shaking hands in my lap and pleaded. "Isn't there anything, anything else I can do?"

"I really don't see what, Teena. And you needn't worry. Your Uncle Charles and Aunt June will be very good to you."

"Perhaps I could take an apartment in Rome," I said hopelessly.

She laughed. "Oh, Teena, really . . ."

"Find some sort of job? Maybe . . ." I let my voice trail away. She raised her eyes to the cloudless blue sky beseeching patience from the heavens. I knew it was no use. I cast about wildly for a more acceptable suggestion, wishing, as I had wished so many times through so many years, that she and Ben had stayed together. And then I thought: Ben. Of course. Ben was my father, after all. I said, "Listen, Margaretha, why don't we get in touch with Ben?"

Her hot blue eyes flashed to my face. She said sharply, "What?"

"Ben," I said, suddenly hesitant. "I could . . ."

"Your father has no interest in you at all," she said deliberately. "I'm surprised that you haven't managed to figure that out after all these years of silence. I haven't the faintest idea of where he is, or what. I haven't the faintest intention of inquiring. As I told you, everything is arranged. You're going to live with the Rentlows. They'll meet you at the airport in Boston." She slipped her dark glasses over her eyes, rose. "I have quite a few things to do, Teena. And so have you. Shall we get started right now?"

I knew that further discussion was useless. I had learned long before that once Margaretha had made up her mind she would have her way.

She said more gently, "I realize that this comes as a bit of a surprise to you. But even though you are remarkably childish in some ways, you're surely grown up enough to know what marrying Timothy means to me. And to you, of course. And going to the Rentlows is what I want you to do."

The next four days spun away in a flurry of preparation. Margaretha and Timothy were married in a small, private ceremony. Afterward, Timothy hugged me, looked down at me ruefully. "Look at the size of those brown eyes, Margaretha. I do think the child is frightened to death." And Margaretha, smiling sweetly, said, "But she isn't a child, Timothy."

I remember thinking it was odd that her view of me shifted to conform to what she wanted. I was too young to live alone, to find a job. But I was grown up, mature

11

enough to do without her apron strings. I wished that some time she would look beneath my face to the real me.

She went on, "We'll write, Teena, the moment we have an address. You must let us know how things are."

Soon after, she and Timothy left on the first leg of their journey to South America.

That same evening, Maria and Tony saw me off, with many anxious instructions and worried reassurances, from Rome Airport.

I fell into the seat to which the smiling stewardess had led me, crushed into taut-throated silence, fainthearted and unwilling, and with a dozen small terrors already assaulting me, and a dozen self-reproaches already burdening me.

I was frightened that my luggage would be lost, my passport stolen. I didn't know how to manage the plane change in London. I didn't know what to do if no one met me in Boston.

Sternly I told myself that I ought to have done something practical. Run away perhaps. Disappeared into the alleys of Rome. Found a job. Learned to live my own life. Why, oh, why hadn't I tried?

And then, as the big jet taxied down the field and made a great leap for the twilight sky over Rome, the stewardess returned to me, leaned across my seat mate, and asked, "Miss Halliday? You *are* Miss Teena Halliday, aren't you?"

I murmured a hesitant acknowledgment.

She put a slip of paper into my hand. "This is a cable for you. It was received at the airport and delivered to the plane just before we took off."

My fingers shook as I accepted it. I unfolded it quickly. It was seconds before I could read it. The block letters seemed to slip and blur, and sudden hot hope, that Margaretha had changed her mind and was wiring me to meet her somewhere, threw a dancing misty veil over the words. But then my vision cleared. The single sentence, and its meaning, touched me with unexpected magic. Sudden hot hope was forgotten, and I read, read over and over again, TEENA DEAR I WILL BE WAITING FOR YOU

AT LOGAN AIRPORT IN BOSTON LOVE YOUR FATHER BEN.

It was a miracle come out of misfortune. The turmoil and terror of the past four days was gone into swift sweet excitement. A twelve-year-old dream was coming true.

"Obviously good news," my seat mate grinned.

I glanced at him. He was a middle-aged man, gray-haired and gray-eyed, surely not one of those dangerous types about whom Maria and Tony had warned me.

"Yes," I told him firmly, "very good news."

"From your boyfriend?" he teased.

I felt hot color sweep into my face. "From my father," I said, and managed to end the conversation by leaning back, eyes closed, while I savored my joy.

The jet skimmed into fiery sunset, then through it into utter darkness.

I ate meagerly of the food the stewardess brought me. I absently answered my seat mate's casual comments. All the while I felt as if I were flying on my own wings, my thoughts speeding giddily through the hours.

My small fears and self-reproaches forgotten, I looked ahead only to meeting Ben.

What would my father look like now?

I remembered him as tall, slim. A laughing man, dimples deep in his square face, with eyes brown and tilted under heavy dark brows as my own, and with thick hair the same golden as my own.

Would he be the same after the twelve intervening years? Or would he have grown fat, old? Would I even know him? I wondered suddenly.

And he, would he know me?

My heart seemed to pound against my ribs. What would he think of me? Would he be satisfied and proud, or disappointed? Would he love me as I knew he once had?

Margaretha had always said he didn't care about me, that never, since the divorce, had he written her, questioned her, asked to see me. I hadn't been able to accept her too-casual comments. I'd always believed there was something that would explain the appearance of his disinterest. And now the miracle of the cable proved

13

Margaretha wrong. Ben *did* care. He was going to meet me. We would be together.

It was only much later that I began to wonder how he knew I would be on that plane, would be arriving at Logan Airport in Boston, how he knew about Margaretha's marriage to Timothy, and that I was coming to live with the Rentlows. Then, as the plane raced through the sky, I thought only of the impression I would make on him; faint apprehension an alloy of my happiness.

I was glad that I had long golden hair, pleased now, that I had tilted brown eyes with long dark curling lashes. For the first time I could remember I stopped envying Margaretha's hot blue gaze. Brown was like Ben. And I knew it was a good thing that I had allowed Maria to talk me into wearing the short white dress, cut in the Rome style, and the tiny white shoes, that I had accepted the extra pair of white gloves for my purse, so that when I finally arrived, I would have clean ones to put on.

I was glad that I was small, slender, because that perhaps would help Ben recall the younger Teena that he had known.

The hours sped by.

I made the change of planes in London without incident, and flew into dawn finally, with my thoughts still leaping ahead, while the smiling stewardesses moved quickly up and down the aisles, and the other passengers rose and stretched and chattered around me.

At last, in midafternoon, the intercom suddenly crackled and coughed, and then a slow but crisp voice announced, "Ladies and gentlemen, this is your captain speaking. We are now moving into a holding pattern over Logan International Airport. Air Traffic control reports that we should be able to land within forty-five minutes. It is four o'clock in Boston. The temperature is a warm August ninety degrees. It is cloudy with a chance of thunderstorms."

"Thunderstorms," my new seat mate said sourly. "Wouldn't you know it? Whenever I land in Boston there's thunderstorms."

I smiled at him vaguely. I had hardly spoken to him since he had sat next to me in London. I had been too

14

busy anticipating the moment when I would see Ben. I leaned back and closed my eyes, sheltering in silent privacy to savor my joy. Soon, I thought. Soon I would see my father.

I didn't know how the miracle had happened, and I didn't think to question it then.

Ben would be there, waiting for me.

It was not all going to be the way I had feared when Margaretha announced her plans.

I was going to my father. Not a family of strangers, an uncle and aunt I didn't remember, cousins I had never seen. I would not be alone and lost in a country that I hardly knew.

At last the plane slid smoothly onto the field and rolled to a stop.

I had gathered my white topcoat, my flight bag. As soon as the doors were opened, I hurried out, eagerly following the other passengers through the routine of landing. I went through passport control, picked up my luggage at Customs, waited while it was inspected and passed. All the while I searched the faces of the milling people around me, seeking a familiar one.

With the routine behind me finally, I dragged my two suitcases beyond the barrier and into the huge crowded waiting room, certain that I would find my father as anxiously searching as I was.

I stayed close to the flight gate at which I had landed, hopefully studying every man that passed by.

Slowly, oh, so slowly, the crowd thinned, and I found myself hopefully looking into faces that I had looked into before.

It was a long time before I admitted to myself what had been a growing, an overwhelming suspicion. With sinking heart, I allowed myself to face the truth.

My father wasn't there.

He wasn't going to come.

15

CHAPTER TWO

Heartsick with disappointment, shivery with slowly growing fear, I concentrated all my heart and mind on seeing my father.

Perhaps that's why it was long moments before I finally remembered that Margaretha had told me very positively that the Rentlows would meet me.

Ben wasn't there. But the Rentlows must be.

Once again I began a slow careful search of the few remaining faces in the waiting room. I told myself that surely, if they were there, they would have guessed that I must be Teena Halliday. I told myself that surely they were as anxiously looking for me as I was now looking for them.

But no one came forward to offer me a greeting, a smile.

I waited, swept by a wave of painful loneliness for the known and familiar, the clatter of swift Italian, the flash of bright open grins. I was uneasily aware of my inexperience, my vulnerability, with Maria's and Tony's nervous warnings still ringing in my ears. I waited, and wondered what I should do.

I had the Rentlows' address and telephone number in my purse. I would, I decided, have to call them, find out what had happened.

With sinking heart, I realized that I had no American money. I didn't even know how to use an American telephone.

It came to me sharply then just how much I really was a stranger in my native land.

I fought back a sudden need to cry, and took myself in hand. I was on my own now. I must learn to cope.

Frightened or not, I must learn. There would be someplace where I could exchange lire for dollars. There would be someone to ask about the telephone.

I couldn't manage to carry my luggage as well as my flight bag and coat, and as I hesitated, looking hopefully for a porter, a tall, red-headed man rushed into the waiting room, surveyed it quickly in a sweeping glance, and with hardly a hitch in his long stride, hurried directly to me.

"Are you Teena Halliday?" he demanded.

I nodded, weak with relief. Someone was there to meet me, help me. He would know what had happened. He would know what I should do.

"I'm Rory Calvert," he said. "Forgive me for not being here when you got off the plane. I had trouble finding a place in the parking lot. It was mobbed, and I had to keep going around in circles. I was scared that you wouldn't . . ."

"It's the same in Rome," I said. "Too many cars, always in the same place at the same time. I'm sorry you had so much trouble."

His eyes were a clear, sharp green. They swept me with a slow appraising look, then narrowed with laughter. "You should be chewing me out," he said, "for keeping you waiting, not apologizing to me, Teena Halliday."

I shrugged that away. I had something else on my mind. "Where is my father?" I asked anxiously. "What happened? Why isn't he here?"

Rory Calvert's green eyes were blank. "Your father?"

"Ben Halliday. He sent me a cable at Rome. It said he'd be here to meet me when I landed."

"I don't know anything about that," Rory said. "I'm a friend and neighbor of the Rentlows. They were unable to drive in today as they'd promised your mother, so I offered to come for you in their stead." He gave me a sudden smile, his eyes meeting mine. "And I'm glad I did." And then, sobering peculiarly, he said, "Yes. I really am, Teena."

"But what happened to my father then?" I asked worriedly, taking the much-handled cable from my purse. "You see? Here it is. You can read it for yourself."

He gave it a quick look, shrugged. "Teena, I'm sorry. I've never heard of Ben Halliday. I don't know anything about him. All I know is that the Rentlows expect me to drive you back to Rentlow Retreat, and if we're to get there before dark we had better get started right now."

There seemed to be nothing to do but go with him. I

17

gave the nearly empty waiting room a last long searching look. He took up my luggage, and I followed him through a maze of corridors and tunnels, up escalators and down them, through a vast field of cars, until at last he led me to a huge blue one, settled me inside it, and threw my bags into the trunk. Moments later, we were on our way.

Boston traffic seemed much like Rome traffic to me, except that so many of the cars were great huge things like Rory's.

Though his big capable hands seemed extremely assured, I was relieved when we turned, at last, into a much less traveled highway and headed, as he explained to me, northward and to the sea.

"It's quite a good ride," he told me. "Rentlow Retreat is actually very isolated. It's about six miles from Tumlee. That's the nearest town. And it's up high on a cliff, overlooking the ocean."

I nodded absently, less concerned with the situation and location of the house then than I was with the Rentlows themselves. Finally I said, "I'm a little surprised that my aunt and uncle weren't able to meet me after all. Margaretha was so definite."

"Margaretha?"

"My mother."

"You always call her by her first name?"

It was none of his business, of course, and I resented the disapproval in his tone, but I found myself explaining stiffly, "She insists on it." Then I tried once more to lead him to explain the Rentlows' absence. "I was certain they'd be at the airport."

"You were certain your father would too, I gather," Rory retorted.

"I thought . . . perhaps . . . in place of them . . . But now that he wasn't . . . it seems . . ."

"I'll explain it later." He gave me a wide warm grin. "Teena, I hope you don't think I'm an impostor, come to steal you away."

That thought was one that hadn't occurred to me. I considered it only briefly, then shook my head. "No. I'm sure that you're not."

"Good. But what makes you sure?"

18

Startled, I turned to him. His green eyes were again narrowed with laughter. I admitted finally, "I don't know," and let it go at that.

But I knew that something in the look of him simply made him seem trustworthy to me. His red hair was short-clipped, and in the stormy light of out-of-doors, actually a sun-burnished auburn. His face was tanned, very rugged, big-jawed, and with a strong jutting nose and high cheekbones. In repose his lips seemed firm, compressed, with a hint of sadness in their dented corners, but when he smiled, they softened with an odd gentleness.

He smiled now, saying, "As long as you don't think I'm an impostor, suppose you lean back and enjoy the trip."

I tried to. I let the hot wind tousle my hair, feeling the smoggy dampness that I knew must presage the thunderstorms the plane's captain had mentioned. I looked at the great pile up of dark clouds gathering on the horizon. I watched the countryside, so different in shape and color from what I was used to, spin past the open window.

I found myself remembering how Margaretha had always insisted that Ben cared nothing for me, and wondering why he had bothered to send me a cable saying he would meet me when he plainly hadn't intended to.

And then suddenly I found myself wondering how he would have known I would be arriving at Logan Airport, on that day, on that plane, in Boston. Someone must have told him. Surely it hadn't been Margaretha. She had had no contact with Ben in years. She had said she had no idea where he was, or what he was doing. It was plain then that he must have learned about my arrival through the Rentlows. There was no one else. They must have been in contact with him, must have told him. And he planned to meet me. But something had delayed him, or deterred him. Just as the Rentlows themselves had been, and sent Rory Calvert instead.

I suddenly found myself light-headed with relief. Why had I been so afraid? Obviously the Rentlows would know all about Ben. Perhaps he was even at Rentlow

Retreat, waiting for this trip to be concluded as eagerly as I was.

Rory broke into my jubilant thoughts, asking, "Teena, you don't mind if I ask you how old you are, do you?"

I slid a look at him, suppressing a sigh. "Not if you don't mind my asking the question back."

A momentary grin touched his lips. "I'm twenty-seven."

"Eighteen," I admitted.

"All of eighteen." His grin faded. "And you've lived most of your life in Italy?"

"Since I was six."

"How was that, Teena?"

I preferred not to talk about it, but I didn't quite know how to refuse to answer without being unacceptably rude. I said finally, "My parents divorced. Margaretha married a man named Arthur Haines, and we three moved to a villa on the Riviera."

"And you've never been back to the States before this?"

I shook my head.

"Then you've never met the Rentlows. You don't know Jeremy or Estrella? Nor remember your Aunt June or your Uncle Charles?"

I shook my head again.

"Has your mother seen them in recent years?"

"No. She hasn't been back either."

"Then how come, now, after all this time, you're . . ."

I sighed, folded my hands in my lap. "Margaretha is off on her honeymoon."

"But . . ."

"She divorced Arthur Haines quite a long time ago. This is Timothy Bye. They're in South America by now, I suppose."

"I see," Rory said thoughtfully. "Then that's why you've come to stay with the Rentlows."

I nodded without answering him. I had begun to wonder why he asked so many questions about something which could hardly concern him, even if he were a family friend.

He persisted, "And you'll be staying for how long?"

20

"Perhaps for six months," I said shortly.

He ignored my obvious curtness. "Why did you have to come here?"

"It was what Margaretha wanted," I told him, as if that explained everything. Which, of course, in a way, it did.

"Still, you could have stayed on in Italy. Closer to your friends, your home," he said, plainly not impressed by Margaretha's desires. "That way there wouldn't have been so many sudden and difficult changes in your life." He was silent for a moment.

I became uneasily aware that his green eyes had shifted from the road to study my face. He stared at me for a long unsmiling time. Then he said, "I expect your mother realized that you weren't really quite ready to go it on your own, and the Rentlows was the answer she came up with."

I felt a hot blush burn my cheeks.

Rory said quickly, "Please don't be offended, Teena. I'm not implying that you're stupid, or dimwitted."

"Thank you for that," I retorted.

"But I am implying that you're highly inexperienced, and very young."

Once again the hot blush burned my cheeks. I said tartly, "That is a condition which time will rectify."

He agreed soberly. "Yes, of course. But until then, please promise me that you'll be careful, that you'll not allow yourself to be swept away by . . . by anything, that you'll give yourself a chance to grow a little more before you . . . before you make any serious commitments in your life."

"I don't know what you're talking about," I told him.

He sighed, stared at the highway ahead. "No, of course you don't. And maybe I don't either. But promise anyway."

He had been kind enough to meet me, even though he was nothing to me, nor I to him. I supposed that his advice was well meant though I didn't particularly welcome it. I smiled. "All right, Rory. I promise I'll grow up before I do anything rash."

Oddly, he neither glanced at me, nor returned my

21

smile. He said, "And one other thing, Teena. If you should be . . . let's say troubled, concerned . . . if anything happens to cause you worry, please trust me. Tell me about it. Think of me as a friend."

I had had very few friends in my life, and I had never warmed quickly to strangers. But as I considered his softly spoken words, I was surprised to find that I somehow could accept him as someone I had known for a long long time. Momentarily, I was warmed by the thought.

"Thank you, Rory," I said. "I'll think of you as a friend."

Even as I said the words I became uneasily aware of what could only be implicit warning in what he had been saying. Why else had he asked that I not commit myself? To what? To whom? Why else had he thought I might be troubled, concerned? Might need a friend? What danger did he see ahead of me?

In spite of the damp hot air I suddenly felt cold.

"Tell me about your father," Rory said.

I explained as briefly as I could.

He frowned, "Then you've never been in contact with him? Not until you received the cable?"

"That's right." I went on, "But I'm sure the Rentlows will know. Tell me about them, Rory."

"You'll see for yourself in a little while. I'll let you be the judge."

I was more certain than ever that I would willingly forego that pleasure. But I reminded myself that Ben would most probably be with them, waiting for me. With Ben there, it would be all right.

And if he wasn't there, I decided suddenly, then as soon as I had Margaretha's mailing address, I would cable her, and tell her what had happened, and ask if she had an explanation.

"I'm the Rentlows' nearest neighbor," Rory was saying. "And that's not very near—two miles by the road. Though there is a rough, ten-minute shortcut along the ridge. I'll show it to you sometime."

"You've known them a long while then?"

He nodded. "And I see a good bit of them. When I'm

not working. I'm an accountant. My office is in my home, and I handle accounts in Tumlee and all the small towns around. They keep me hopping. Which is just as well, now that I live alone."

The slight change in his voice made the last four words seem somehow significant. I asked myself what it meant.

He must have caught the expression on my face, for he asked, "What's wrong? Are you wondering why I'm an accountant?"

"Oh, no."

"Then?"

"I suppose I was wondering why you worked at anything," I told him. "Most of the people I knew at home didn't, you see."

He grinned as he shook his head.

I fell silent, thinking about the Rentlows. Margaretha had spoken of Aunt Jane and Uncle Charles so rarely. That in itself suddenly seemed odd to me. I'd learned more of them in those few comments she'd made when she told me I'd be going to live with them than in all the years before. Yet even that had been a strangely brief account.

Rory made a sharp right turn. The road began to twist and climb, steep banks of stone suddenly rising on both sides of us, and only a narrow ribbon of twilight and cloud-darkened sky above.

He said, "Well, here, most of the people you'll meet will work at something."

"And my Uncle Charles?"

"The Rentlows have inherited income," Rory said shortly.

Then my Uncle Charles had managed even though disappointed that my Aunt June had no money of her own.

Rory was saying, "So I keep house, and cook, and I'm a pretty fair one, if I do say so myself."

I imagined, taking a quick glance at his competent hands again, that he was good at whatever he set out to do. I didn't know why. He just struck me that way.

He made another sharp turn, and the road became a rocky unpaved lane. Within moments, he drew up before

...tall spiked iron gate that closed an opening in a high stone wall.

A small tan car was parked at one side.

"Right on time," Rory muttered, and got out so quickly that I had no opportunity to ask him what he meant.

As he strode toward the gate, it swung open.

A short, plump woman scurried through it. It slammed behind her with a loud, metallic clang.

Rory paused to talk to her for a moment. Then she climbed stiffly into the small car. It spun around, passed me quickly and disappeared down the lane.

Meanwhile Rory had gone to the gate, raised his hand to operate a mechanism I couldn't see, and then rejoined me.

"It's always kept locked," he explained as the tall gate swung open and he drove us through. "There's a release in the house that opens it."

The locked gate didn't surprise me. Most of the villas in Italy had them too. It was weeks before I realized what horror those locked gates would come to mean to me.

I leaned foward, peering ahead through the murky shadows cast by the huge leafy oak trees that arched over the lane. Sudden gusts of wind shook them, and they swayed, exposing bits of storm-green sky and swirling black clouds.

On our left there was a huge grove of what appeared to be tall hedges.

"A maze," Rory said, seeing the quick wondering glance that I gave it. "Very old, done a long long time ago, except for some recent additions over the years."

I noted the sound of strain in his voice, asked, "You don't like the additions?"

He ignored the question, said, "The lady you saw leaving just now. That is Mrs. Foxall, the housekeeper. Her husband always picks her up this time of day."

"Oh, that's what you meant when you said 'Right on time,' before."

He nodded. "You can set your watch by her."

On our right there was a smooth, well-kept lawn. As we drove past it, the storm-green sky seemed to split open with a huge flash of lightning and a roar of thunder. Rain suddenly poured down on us, a thick, wind-driven slanting rain that curtained our surroundings. Through it I had a glimpse of movement on the smooth lawn. I saw a faun leap. I saw an owl fly. I saw a dog rise up, his tail wagging. And then the wind must have changed, for the rain slanted a different way. I realized that I was staring at stone figures, statuary that could hardly have moved.

A slow cold shiver went over me. I found myself swallowing hard. I blurted, "Rory, I could have sworn all that statuary was actually moving. I could have sworn those figures were real, and running and playing in the rain."

Rory slowed the car, allowed it to drift to a stop. "Maybe they were once alive, Teena. Things aren't always what they seem, you know. Be careful in Rentlow Retreat. And remember your promise to me. Remember that I'm your friend."

Once again I recognized his words to be a sober warning. But against what I still didn't know.

There was no time for me to consider it further then, no time even to question him.

I could think of nothing beyond the fact that within moments I would see Ben. I would throw myself into my father's arms. And then all my questions would be answered.

Rory had parked before a wide, wind-swept terrace. Beyond it I saw the big stone house. The huge wooden door swung open on yellow lamplight. It appeared to shrink and flicker under the lash of wind and rain, under the blanket of greenish sky.

The rain thinned, stopped as suddenly as it had begun. The wind blew harder.

Four figures came outside and waited motionlessly.

Wind-whipped, dressed in black, they seemed to hunch like hungry vultures over their unsuspecting prey.

I wished Rory would turn the car and drive away as fast as he could.

But he said gently, "Rentlow Retreat, Teena. They're waiting for you."

25

I wished that I dared climb from the car, and flee into the fast-falling darkness.

Instead, reminding myself that Ben must be here, I got out, hurried across the terrace.

There were two men and two women. I saw their faces in the dim light that showed through the open door.

Even as I approached them, I knew that Ben was not with them, and as I looked from face to face, I was aware of an odd blankness, a emptiness, a braced withholding that could never be mistaken for welcome.

"But what's the matter?" I cried, before I could stop myself. "Didn't you really expect me?" And then, "And where's my father? Why isn't he here to meet me?"

CHAPTER THREE

For a moment the four figures seemed frozen, immobile. They might have been the statuary Rory and I had just passed by. A group of carved bodies, dressed in mourning black.

Rory had said he would tell me why the Rentlows had not been at the airport to meet me. He had not had to. Seeing them, I knew. They were dressed in mourning black.

There had been a death.

Four rigid bodies waited. Four sets of eyes regarded me without expression.

And then lightning flashed. Thunder rolled. The big wooden door slammed shut and then slammed open.

I was surrounded by quick moving figures that drew me inside, engulfed in a scatter of exclamations that only confused me.

I stood in the huge foyer, shivering in the electric heat of an August storm, and looked anxiously from face to face.

"Of course we expected you, Teena."

"How was your trip?"

"We're so glad to have you here."

"Did Rory find you all right?"

The questions swirled around me in peculiar cross

currents. I had no chance to reply. I obviously wasn't expected to. I had the strange feeling that all the words were simply a kind of background music to a scene being played out before me, a scene for my benefit, yet one in which I was a central figure, without knowing my role.

Aunt June was tall, gaunt. Although I knew she was just two years older than Margaretha, she seemed a a woman far along into middle age. Her hair was gray-streaked, and drawn back from her thin face in a tight high bun. Her blue eyes were pale, as if washed clean of color by too many tears. The plain black dress she wore was loose at the waist and throat, and hung unevenly at the hem. She put out a thin, shaking hand, said, "Teena, dear child, I am so happy to see you at last."

I could see no happiness in the tight clench of tension in her face, nor hear any sound of it in her faltering voice. My heart sank. I knew Aunt June hadn't wanted me to come to Rentlow Retreat.

Uncle Charles was tall, portly, his shoulders as wide as a wall in his black suit. His cold gray eyes studied me from behind thick rimless glasses. "I don't see any resemblance to Margaretha," he said at last. "Which is just as well, I suppose."

I was startled at my sudden amusement. Uncle Charles, I gathered, still resented Margaretha's rejection of him so long before. I supposed that was why his square red face offered me no more welcome than his words had.

"Hi there, Teena," Estrella said, her breathtakingly beautiful face impassive, with no warmth in her voice nor smile in her dark eyes.

Jeremy stood very still, his head bent, his face blank with total concentration. Margaretha had said he was twenty-four, but he seemed older than that to me. His hair was very dark and wavy, and grew in a beautifully defined widow's peak. His brows were thick and dark too, and under them, his very dark eyes seemed to glitter with chips of light. I thought he was the most handsome man I had ever seen, yet at the same time, something about him repelled me. But suddenly he smiled and said, "We were wondering what to expect. And now we know."

27

Rory moved restively beside me.

Jeremy continued to stare at me, and I found myself growing uncomfortable under the intensity of his look.

Then, a small sound broke the silence that had fallen, and we all looked toward the stairs.

A small white dog came down slowly, panting as it made its way.

"Scuffy!" Jeremy said. "What are you doing here?"

"Poor Scuffy," Estrella muttered, "you want to be where the company is, don't you?"

"What's the matter with him?" Rory asked. "He looks sick."

Aunt Jane and Estrella both began to speak at the same time. Jeremy's voice overrode theirs.

"I guess Scuffy's just getting old."

"He was okay the last time I saw him," Rory said. He bent, whistled softly, and the white dog made a wide circle around Jeremy and dragged himself to Rory's feet. Rory picked him up, frowned. "He'd better see a vet, Jeremy."

"Maybe you're right. I'll take him in tomorrow."

Once again a small silence fell. Then Aunt June suggested that I might like to go to my room, to get settled down and change after my journey. The others enthusiastically agreed that was a good idea, and the group began to break up.

But I said, "Wait." My eyes swept the big foyer, peered past wide open double doors to the room I saw beyond. "Wait a minute. I asked you before, don't you remember? Where's Ben? Where's my father?"

Dim light glimmered on Uncle Charles' rimless glasses, obscuring his gray eyes. A ripple of bewilderment broke his stolid, heavily scored red face. "I thought I heard you ask that when you came up to the terrace. But I assumed that I had somehow misunderstood you, Teena. Why should you ask us about Ben Halliday?"

I was wordless with disappointment. I found myself looking hopefully from face to face, praying that I had only imagined Charles' words, that it was a joke, and he was teasing, and in a moment, Ben would come bounding to meet me.

28

Instead, Rory explained quickly about the cable that I had received.

"I'm so sorry for you," Aunt June said. "How sad this should have happened."

"But we know nothing of Ben Halliday," Charles cut in, his voice low and hard, and angry. "We haven't heard from him since the day your mother left him, Teena. We haven't seen him since that day. And that's been twelve long years ago."

I looked disbelievingly at Charles. He met my gaze implacably. I looked at June. She shook her gray-streaked head. I looked at Estrella. She turned away, took Rory's arm, tilting her beautiful face up to his.

Jeremy said gently, "There's been a mistake of some kind, Teena. For now you must make yourself at home, and we'll get it all straightened out later on."

Aunt June led me upstairs. "Jeremy's quite right. We'll straighten it out later on."

I think I realized, even then, that what I had thought of as my own special miracle would not come to pass after all. I think I knew I was not fated to see my father. But I wouldn't allow myself to believe that. I clung to Jeremy's suggestion that there had been some mistake, misunderstanding, that would soon be cleared up.

As soon as Aunt June left me alone in my room, I took out the much-handled cable, read it again. No. There was no error. Ben had said he would meet me. But he had not. I decided that he had been delayed. Still, he must know where I was going. He must know where he could find me.

I wondered, though, how, if he hadn't seen nor heard from the Rentlows for twelve years, he had known I would be coming to stay with them. It was a puzzle I couldn't solve. I shrugged the question away. He would answer it when he arrived. And it would be soon, I told myself. Of course it would be soon. He knew I was waiting for him.

My room was on the third floor. It was large, well-decorated, with heavy green drapes at the two windows, and a thick soft carpet on the floor in the same shade of green. The furniture was old-fashioned, dark and squat, but it shone with care and polish. There was a fireplace set under a white marble mantel, and above it a huge gold-framed mirror. Within it, from across the room, I saw my pinched white face. I turned quickly away from it, unwilling to face its woebegone aspect.

I had unpacked, finished putting my things away, and changed to a pink dress with a full skirt and high stand-up collar, and to narrow-heeled pink sandals, when Jeremy came for me.

From outside the closed door, I heard him call, "Teena? Ready now?"

I went out to him. "I hope I wasn't too long."

"Of course not," he said, smiling at me. "You've changed your clothes. How nice you look, Teena."

I was disconcerted by the piercing intensity with which he looked down at me. He seemed to know that. His smile widened. He touched my cheek. "I'm glad you're here. You will be too. Just wait and see."

I didn't answer him, but I knew that I would do exactly that.

We went downstairs together. Jeremy led me into the room where the rest of the family had gathered.

My earlier glimpse of it had not prepared me for its dark and heavy elegance. Every inch of the floor was covered with opulent Oriental carpeting. The walls were hung with pale tapestries. The furniture was large and deep and soft, done in silken coverings. The lamps were tall and slim, enameled with minute figures. The high marble mantel displayed a group of small satiny stone statues.

It was surely a beautiful place, rich in every detail, yet overlaid with an odd air of shabbiness. I realized suddenly that there were worn places in the fine Oriental rugs, that the hangings had been carefully repaired. Everything was well cared for, but aged with long use, and used long after wealth would have replaced it.

"Are you settled?" Aunt June asked. "Did you find everything that you need?"

I told her that I had.

"And do you think you'll be comfortable? If not, we can find you another room, Teena. We do want you to feel at home."

"I'll be fine," I said quickly, taking a chair closest to where I stood, while Jeremy sat down nearby.

Rory, I saw, was watching me, green eyes narrowed. I was sure that he was trying to assess my reaction to the Rentlows.

I was relieved when his attention was diverted from me by Scuffy's careful sidling walk. The small white dog once again made a wide circle around Jeremy and went to lean tiredly at Rory's feet. He turned his narrowed green eyes on Scuffy, and patted the dog gently.

Estrella had been busy at the long coffee table. She offered me a cup of coffee, her dark shining glance sliding past me to touch on Rory.

I accepted some, trying not to see the overt hunger in her gaze.

"We live so quietly here," Aunt June said, breaking what had become a long uncomfortable silence. "I hope it will do for you, Teena."

"I'm accustomed to that," I told her.

"Oh? Why, I thought that in Italy, surely, it was all very, very gay."

I supposed that it was, for some people. For Margaretha, in fact, life had certainly been exciting. She was always on the go, seeing friends, partying, taking small trips. But I had never been part of that social whirl. I hadn't wanted to be. And in that, I had had my way. I had spent most of my time at the villa with plump Maria and hard-working Tony. I saw no reason to explain that to Aunt June, however, so I simply smiled at her.

"Perhaps I was wrong then," she shrugged.

Charles put in heavily, "You always permit your imagination to run away with you, June. And that's just one more instance."

I sensed a meaning in the reproach which I didn't understand, and looking at the statues on the mantel, found an excuse to change the subject. "Those are nice," I told Jeremy. "Where do they come from?"

His dark eyes glinted at me, heavy brows peaking. "From me, Teena. I do them. I've done all the sculpture you see in and around the house."

31

"What a wonderful talent," I said, knowing it an inane comment, but having no other to offer.

He leaned closer to me, smiling. "Some day I shall do you, Teena. And soon."

Estrella said quickly, "Teena, you must tell me all about your trip. I've never been lucky enough to travel. I'm always stuck here. So . . ."

"It was pleasant." I looked at her helplessly. I didn't know what more to say. The journey hadn't mattered to me. I had been looking ahead to seeing Ben. Looking ahead to nothing, I knew now. I told myself hurriedly that I mustn't give up. He had known I was coming here. He would know how to find me.

"I think I'd better get home now," Rory said suddenly, and rose to his feet.

Scuffy whimpered, rubbed against his ankles.

Jeremy whistled softly, but the white dog came limping to me. I lifted him, held his too-thin, quivering body in my lap.

Estrella wailed, "Rory, oh, no, why I've had hardly a minute to talk to you, and you were away all last week too. The least you could do . . ."

He grinned. "That's why I think I should go home. I have enough work for the whole evening and the night too. I'll see you tomorrow, Estrella."

"But tomorrow's so far away," she insisted. "Now, please, you must, you absolutely must pamper me. Please, Rory, just for a little while."

But he grinned and shook his auburn head. He crossed the room to stand over me. "I'll see you tomorrow too," he told me, and then, wordlessly, but eloquently, his green eyes reminded me of the promise I had made to him.

I thanked him for meeting me at the airport, for driving me to Rentlow Retreat, and added, knowing he would understand, "I appreciate all your help, Rory."

When he had gone, with Estrella still trailing after him, the big room seemed even colder. It was as if a small flame of warmth had gone out with him.

The others sat in heavy silence, still regarding me with peculiarly watchful eyes.

Finally, uncomfortable and anxious, I said, "I hope

32

that my coming here isn't an intrusion. Perhaps it's an inconvenient time for you, or perhaps . . ."

"Of course not," Aunt June said quickly. "My dear, you mustn't think that." Her washed-out blue eyes flickered between Uncle Charles and Jeremy, as if asking for help.

Uncle Charles' rimless glasses flashed me a blank look. "Why do you say that? Why should it be an inconvenient time?"

"I just thought . . ."

Jeremy saved me from having to finish a sentence that I didn't know how to finish. He grinned, "We're glad you're here. You'll never know how glad. We needed a breath of fresh air in Rentlow Retreat. We've all been sinking in our own swamps, and now, with you . . ."

Aunt June fluttered a gaunt hand. "Oh, Teena, dear child, I'm afraid I know what you're thinking. It's because we weren't at the airport as we'd promised. It wasn't because we didn't want to be, dear. You mustn't think that, you mustn't think you're unwelcome. It's not that. Not at all. But you see . . ."

"Something happened," Uncle Charles said heavily.

I knew what he was going to say. I knew someone had died. They were all dressed in mourning black.

He went on, "We had a death, you see. A close friend. A guest in our house. The services were today, Teena."

"I'm sorry," I murmured.

"There was nothing any of us could do, of course," Uncle Charles told me. "Fortunately Rory was just back from his trip, so he was able to do us the favor . . ." Uncle Charles rose. "And now if you'll excuse me. I have some things to attend to in my study."

Without waiting for an answer, he walked heavily across the room, disappeared into the shadows of the foyer.

"I must think about dinner," Aunt June told me. She smiled faintly, and I saw an echo of my mother's smile in her face, but just an echo, faint and pale and somehow pathetic. "I imagine that you're accustomed to dozens of servants. But we don't . . . we don't do things that way in this country, of course. We have day help, but no one lives in."

"Perhaps there's something I can do," I offered.

"Oh, no," she said hastily, and turned to Jeremy. "You might check around and be sure that the storm hasn't done any damage."

He told me he would be back in a little while, and rose with a grace that I realized was characteristic of him. Before he left the room with June, he paused, took Scuffy from my lap. The small dog whimpered as Jeremy lifted him. "Poor old thing," Jeremy said, "he just doesn't know what's happening to him."

"Who does?" Estrella demanded, posing in the doorway. Jeremy brushed by her.

She gave me a quick bright glance. "I guess you're thinking we're the oddest people you've ever seen."

"Oh, no," I protested quickly. "Why should I?"

" 'Why should you?' " she mocked me. "Now, Teena, surely you don't think that I've decided you're deaf, dumb, and blind, as well as stupid too."

"I don't know what you mean."

"If I were you," she told me slowly, "and I'd flown all the way from Italy, expecting to be met by my family, and they didn't show up, and by my father, and he didn't show up, then I'd begin to wonder."

"I did. But then, when your parents explained about the death, and the burial service . . ."

"I'm glad. If you really *do* understand. We were quite frantic about how to handle it. But when Rory turned up and offered . . ."

A light came into her face as she said his name. I was certain then that she cared for him, cared for him deeply and fully, the way a woman can care for a man. The recognition gave me an odd touch of pain. I had no time to examine its cause.

She said, "If it hadn't been for Rory . . . oh, yes, not just today, to pick you up, but so many other times too."

"He's a good friend, isn't he?"

"Oh, yes, that. But what did you think of him, Teena? Truly."

"Why, I don't know," I said cautiously. "He seems very pleasant, and kind, and . . ."

She chuckled. "Maybe you're drawn only to dark-haired types. Like Jeremy."

I blinked at her. "I was thinking in other terms, Estrella."

"When girls meet men they never think in other terms," she told me pleasantly. "And besides, it runs in the family, doesn't it?"

I knew she was making an oblique reference to Margaretha. There had been Charles at first, and then Ben. There had been Arthur Haines, and now there was Timothy Bye. Estrella's comment had a certain amount of justice in it, I supposed, but I didn't know how to answer her. Fortunately I didn't have to.

She said, "Come on, I want to get out of this ridiculous black rig. Let's go up to my room so I can change, and then I'll take you on a tour of Rentlow Retreat."

As I followed her upstairs I wondered what friend and guest of theirs had died. It was an idle thought. I knew it could be no one that I would know.

I followed her down the long hall, passed the door to my room. Hers was a twin to mine, except that the furnishings were done in dark blue instead of in green. She changed quickly from her black dress to blue hip-huggers and a sleeveless blue shirt. She grinned, "You can see that we don't bother to dress for dinner around here. Why should we? Who for?" Without waiting for an answer, she went on, "Except when Rory comes. And then I'll go all out. Naturally." She added softly, "Though I doubt he ever notices."

I doubted that he could fail to. She was an unusually beautiful girl, inherently exotic and exciting. He didn't seem like the type to overlook that. Once again I felt an odd touch of pain. Perhaps I even winced.

"What's wrong?" Estrella demanded.

"Nothing."

"You're still thinking of your father, aren't you, Teena?"

I shook my head.

"It's better not to. You might never find out what happened."

"I have to, though."

35

"You haven't seen him for so long. Why does it matter so much now?"

"He said he'd meet me," I told her, stubbornly clinging to that one fact.

"But he didn't meet you," she said. "He didn't. So that's that."

I couldn't so easily dismiss my disappointment, but I didn't try to explain that to her. I looked casually at a large framed picture that sat on her dresser. It looked faintly familiar to me. A thin-faced blonde girl with wide-apart eyes . . .

Estrella said softly, "That's Sarah Calvert."

"Calvert?" I repeated.

"Rory's sister. We were such good friends." Estrella's dark eyes were suddenly awash with tears. "I miss her. All the time, in every way. The four of us, growing up together, and then, when we were grown . . ."

"But what happened?" I asked.

"She died. It was six months ago, but I . . ."

"So young?"

Estrella turned her back on the picture. "It was one of those things."

Now I understood the oddly significant tone in which Rory told me that he lived alone. He had been thinking of his sister, lost only a little time before.

"Come on," Estrella said. "I'll give you the grand tour. Just follow me."

She drew me from her room, past a closed door. "That's Jeremy's studio. We don't go in there."

The words were hardly said when the door opened. Jeremy stood there, Scuffy tucked under his arm. "Want to come in?"

"Oh, no," Estrella told him quickly. "We're going to do the house. And then it'll be time for dinner, and I'm sure that Teena's exhausted, so . . ."

"Come on," he cut in, stepping back. "Come on, Teena. Estrella, I insist. It'll only take a minute."

I hesitated, but her fingers curled around my arm. She pulled me with her, crying, "Not now. Not now, Jeremy. Don't be such a pest."

36

I heard him laugh, say, "One of these days, I'm going to do a figure of you, Estrella."

"Oh, no, you're not," she said under her breath. And then, turning to me with a wide empty grin, she said, "Brothers!"

But I saw her whole body quiver, and I knew she was afraid of him.

Dinner was an uncomfortable affair.

Uncle Charles sat as if his needs were being attended to by a retinue of servants, while Aunt June and Estrella, refusing my offer of help, brought the food to the table.

Later I learned that the housekeeper, Mrs. Foxall, prepared the evening meal and left it ready before she departed for her home each night, and cleaned up the kitchen the following morning.

Aunt June made sporadic efforts at conversation, with Estrella chiming in. Uncle Charles ate stolidly ignoring us all. Jeremy was silent too, but I was aware of his dark eyes fixed on me in interested contemplation. It was flattering, but unnerving. I was glad when Uncle Charles finally rose, returned to his study. My eyes were heavy with fatigue, my thoughts awhirl. As soon as I decently could, I excused myself and escaped to my room.

There, curled up in bed, with the lights out, I tried to sort out a whole group of confusing impressions, while somewhere down the hall, I could hear Scuffy's unhappy whimpering.

My aunt and uncle had agreed to Margaretha's suggestion that I stay with them for six months, but plainly they didn't really want me. I wondered why they had agreed. I wondered why they didn't want me.

Estrella had been mildly friendly, but I had realized as she led me on the perfunctory tour of the house that her mind had not been on me, but on things I couldn't guess. We'd passed an alcove closed off with a small desk. It had caught my attention because it looked like an antique. When I paused to look at it, she hurried me away. "Oh, that's just some old thing from the garage, to keep people from wandering up to the attic," she'd said. She'd hurried me past her father's study, her mother's sewing room. She'd shrugged finally and told me, "I guess that's the lot. Let's go downstairs now."

Jeremy was the only one who seemed really to care about me, but something in his smile, in the very intensity of his eyes, troubled me.

And Rory . . . he had so plainly warned me of a danger in Rentlow Retreat. But danger of what?

I listened to the wind sigh at the eaves of the silent house, and thought of my father. Where was he? Why hadn't he come? When would I see him?

Awhirl with confused impressions, with unanswered and pressing questions, I finally fell asleep . . .

There was a voice calling to me. *Teena. Teena. Teena.*

I fought my way out of uneasy dreams, straining to listen.

The wind sighed; the house whispered.

But yes. I heard the call again. *Teena. Teena. Teena.*

I sat up, peered around the unfamiliar room.

It took me long moments to remember where I was, to realize that shouting for Maria would bring no answer. Through those long moments I listened to a thick breathless silence.

I decided that I had been dreaming. Strange beds in strange houses were always hard for me to get used to. I leaned back against the pillows, closed my eyes against the unfriendly dark.

Moments later, I heard it again. And that time I was sure. *Teena. Teena. Teena.*

I was fully awake. I wasn't dreaming.

I rose and slipped from the bed.

I eased the door open and peered into the dark empty hall.

Once more I heard the soft whisper of my name.

It was from outside, below.

The heavy drapes billowed out from the partly open window. I went to them, drew them back.

Teena . . .

The big casement window was heavy to my touch. I forced it, flung it wide, and leaned out to peer at the terrace below.

38

Something gave way under my weight. I felt myself slip, fall forward. I grabbed wildly for the drapes and caught them.

My shoulder hit the center casement bar. It snapped. The whole window fell away into the darkness below.

I screamed as the empty night came up to meet me.

CHAPTER FOUR

I screamed, but I had no breath in my lungs with which to make sound.

I struggled, my fingers tangled in the thick strong velvet, but slipping while my weight dangled, head down, blood rushing into my temples and pulses thundering in my ears.

Below me, after the awful clatter of metal and stone and the splintering of glass, there was silence. I saw faint glints of reflected light shift and spin, and I imagined I saw a trail of movement laid down by a drifting shadow.

At last, gasping, at strength's end, I managed to haul myself back up. The velvet drapes were a lifeline to safety. Bruised, still breathless, I found myself on my feet, leaning exhaustedly against the wall, and staring at the wide-open place where the window had been.

Had been.

Because now it was gone, quite gone. The frame, the casement, the center retaining bar were gone. They had snapped out, fallen away into the dark of the night, the moment I touched them.

Fallen away at my touch, I thought, while I leaned forward, hearing a voice whisper *Teena, Teena, Teena,* from below.

I had been sure, without considering it, that Ben had been calling to me. Sure that he had come at last. How I ached to throw myself into his arms.

But Ben's voice had been no more than a voice in a dream.

I found my way back to my bed through the unfamiliar shape of the dark room. I sat hunched on the edge of the mattress, my toes curling in the thick carpet.

The house was wrapped in utter silence. No one was astir.

Had Ben's voice calling to me really been no more than a dream?

My unspoken question seemed a great shout, echoing endlessly, until a second question joined it.

Why had the window fallen away at my touch?

That, too, seemed an unspoken shout, with its own endless echoes.

I peered through the shadows toward the window across the room. It was now no more than a great black rectangle framing the cloud-streaked sky beyond.

The velvet drapes hung crookedly, bunched and sagging, torn from their ceiling moorings by my frantic grasp.

It occurred to me then to wonder why the house had remained so utterly enwrapped in silence after that singular thunder of noise.

At that moment, I heard footsteps in the hall. I snatched a robe, put it on. The door opened slowly, spilling pale light across the carpet.

A dark ominous shadow stood there.

"Who is it?" I gasped, and shrank back.

The ominous shadow moved and became Uncle Charles. "Teena? Are you all right?" His voice was deep, grating, as he went on, "I had a feeling that I heard a loud noise from somewhere. I've checked all the other rooms. Did you . . ."

"Yes. It was in here. The window . . ." I gestured toward the sagging drapes. "When I opened it . . ."

"Opened it?"

The overhead chandelier suddenly bloomed with light. The shadows fled.

Uncle Charles stared first at me, then the window. He belted his dark robe around him more firmly as he strode heavily across the room.

"What is it, Charles? What's happened?" Aunt June cried, peering around the door frame, her haggard face shrunken and gray. "What's the . . ."

"It's a peculiar thing," Uncle Charles told her, not turning from the blank place where the window had been. "The whole frame just fell out. I can't imagine how . . ."

"Fell out?" she shrilled. She came to me swiftly and put a tense arm around my shoulder. "Oh, Teena, child, how frightened you must have been. I'm sorry. Oh, I'm so sorry this had to happen."

Once again I had the fleeting impression that I was watching a performance put on for my benefit, a performance in which I played a part without knowing what that part was.

"I thought it must be thunder far out to sea," Uncle Charles was saying. "But I got up to look anyway. It was hard to tell where the sound came from." He pulled the sagging drapes together. "Ah, well, it can be mended."

"But how . . ."

He gave me a glinting gray look. "I suppose the wind weakened it, loosened the frame . . ."

"An old house," Aunt June murmured. "But, oh, Teena, if you only knew . . ."

She was plainly upset. Her teeth chattered. Her faded blue eyes were anguished. The arm around my shoulder shook.

Uncle Charles said dryly, "June, hysteria won't help. I suggest you go to bed."

And from the doorway, Estrella cried, "But what happened?" She yawned widely. She flung her long dark hair back from her face, and advanced into the room. "What's going on?"

Uncle Charles said irritably, "Nothing, nothing. The wind broke a window and frightened Teena."

I hadn't had a chance to explain that I'd heard a voice call my name outside, that I'd gone to look and leaned against the window frame. I was glad now that I'd said nothing. But I could remember no wind blowing then. I could remember no sound. Just the whisper, *Teena, Teena, Tenna . . .*

"I was just falling asleep," Estrella said. "I thought I was dreaming. But then, everybody talking . . . I realized . . ."

I hadn't heard Jeremy come in. But suddenly he was there, smiling gently at me. "Teena, love, you mustn't get a bad impression of Rentlow Retreat. Even if windows fall out in the night, the house isn't going to fall down."

41

"Oh, no." I tried to smile back at him. I tried to make the tight muscles of my face relax, to wipe away any revealing expression.

He went on, "But how did the drapes get pulled out like that? Surely the wind . . ."

"She must have dragged them down when she went to look at what happened," Uncle Charles said firmly. He raised his voice to overcome Aunt June's wordless gasp. "And I think we should all go back to bed now. Nothing's done that can't be mended. And mended it will be."

He swept the others with him, disappeared down the hall with Aunt June and Jeremy in tow. But Estrella hung back.

When they were gone, the hall dark again, she said, "Teena, I was wondering before, and never asked, but do you have any other relatives? I mean besides us. In this country? Do you have any friends?"

I shook my head slowly. "No. No one at all." I wondered why she wanted to know, but I didn't ask her.

She said slowly, "And you can't get in touch with your mother, can you?"

"Not yet. But I'll have a letter from her soon."

"And there's no one else."

"Just my father," I said softly, thinking of the voice from out of the dark. "Just him."

She flung her hair back again. "Well, you'll be all right. Don't worry about it." Her voice was suddenly brisk, calm. "I guess we'd better go to sleep. Rest well, Teena."

When she had gone, the door closed firmly behind her, the room dark again, I thought of Rory.

He had asked me to think of him as a friend. I wondered if I dare count on him.

But I wasted only a moment on that speculation. I knew that time would give me the answer. I went back to the window, once more drew back the drapes that Uncle Charles had firmly closed.

I had been awakened by a voice calling me from below. I had gone to the window, leaned on it, and it had fallen away from me. I would have fallen with

42

it, onto the stone terrace, except for the heavy velvet that had been my lifeline back to safety.

Had the voice below been a voice in my dreams?

Had the storm really battered the window loose so that my shoulder could easily dislodge it?

I played my fingers over the setting of the metal frame, feeling along crumbled mortar and jagged metal pins until I found the center bar of the casement. It seemed to be sheared smooth. I drew a chair close and climbed up on it, and felt along the top of the frame where the center bar had been attached. Again I found it to be smooth.

I finally returned to my bed. I thought that the window frame had been prepared for my leaning weight. I thought that the voice I had heard had been meant to lure me into falling to my death on the terrace below.

I couldn't be sure. I might have dreamed of Ben calling me. I knew nothing of carpentry. Perhaps my uneasiness at being in Rentlow Retreat, my obstinate feeling that I wasn't really wanted, my own discomfort with strangers, even though they were my relations, made me imagine intent where there had been accident.

But I determined that I would examine the fallen frame by morning light. I would creep down to the terrace at dawn, and see what the remains lying there could tell me.

I realized even then that though my suspicion be confirmed I would still not know the reason behind it, nor the person.

Why should someone at Rentlow want me to die?

If I were not wanted here, then surely a refusal of Margaretha's request would have been in order. The Rentlows owed my mother nothing that I could see. They had only to say it would be inconvenient to have me, and that would have been the end of it. Instead, they had allowed me to come.

And who could have tampered with the window? It seemed to me that any of them would have had ample opportunity, either before I had arrived, or even afterwards. Uncle Charles had been off, he said, in his study.

Jeremy had been checking the house and grounds for storm damage. Estrella and June had been with me and gone a dozen times, and anyway, it somehow seemed to me that dealing with the window would have been a man's job, not a woman's.

But why would Uncle Charles, or Jeremy, want me to die?

I reminded myself that I mustn't jump to conclusions. I didn't know. I wasn't sure. But it was terrible to be alone in the empty dark.

It was hours before I slept.

It wasn't dawn when I awakened, but still early in a beautiful clear sunny day.

I dressed in white trousers, smiling to remember how often Maria objected to me in pants. Everyone wore them, of course, but Maria didn't approve and was voluble on the subject. I fought back an aching wave of homesickness as I pulled on a white shirt, and brushed my hair, then tied it in a red ribbon. I listened at the door, then stepped into the hall. The house was still wrapped in silence. I hurried down to the terrace, relieved that I met no one on the way.

The great sweep of flagstone was littered with fallen leaves flung there by the storm of the night before. Puddles glinted like small mirrors. Except for the carpet of leaves, though, the terrace was bare.

I looked up at the place where the window had been, and it was easy to calculate where it must have fallen. Neither twisted metal frame nor shards of glass marked the place. Unbelievingly I went to the spot. I knelt, touched the cool stone. I felt something prick my fingers and I looked at them. They had two tiny cuts, and I saw the sparkle of splintered glass. I brushed the thin shards carefully away.

As I rose, I realized that someone was staring at me. I turned quickly, my breath suddenly gone.

A short broad woman stood in the open doorway staring at me. She had gray hair drawn into a tight bun. Her face was round, but her cheeks were hollowed. Her eyes were black and sharp, deep-set under a wrinkled

44

brow. She wore a beige dress, heavy black shoes, one of which had an exceptionally thick sole.

It was a moment before I recognized her as Mrs. Foxall, the housekeeper I'd seen leaving the evening before when Rory drove me up to the gates of Rentlow Retreat for the first time.

Now she limped toward me, and the stoniness of her face broke into a shrunken yellow mask, like half a grapefruit skin left too long in the sun.

"I'm Mrs. Foxall," she said. "And you're Teena Halliday. So you got here, after all, did you?"

I agreed that I was, and politely expressed pleasure at meeting her. It was obvious that she felt no pleasure at meeting me, however, and obvious, too, that she wouldn't pretend she did.

Her black eyes studied me. Her pursed lips twitched.

I said, "I came last night, just as you were leaving."

She jerked her head. "That's when I leave. Yes. Always at twilight. I'm not about to hang around. Not when I've a home to go to." She jerked her head again. "And certainly not after dark."

She went on, "But I had a glimpse of you too. And I thought to myself, 'Well, then, she's come after all. More company in the house.' I ought to of known. But after all the talk, that whole week long, I figured that maybe you wouldn't come."

"Talk?" I repeated.

"Talk, talk. The whole bunch of them. And him here too. Though he didn't know if he was coming or going, not if you ask me."

"Him?" I asked.

"The other company," she explained. "Harper. Bethel Harper. That's what his name was. And high as a kite all the time, if you ask me. High on something. Always laughing and kicking up his heels. Good spirits, Charles Rentlow told me. His nature, June Rentlow said. Spirits, maybe, I thought to myself. But if so, out of a bottle, though I can't actually say I saw him drink. Or the dope maybe. Though again, I can't say for sure. Whatever it was, he had it. That Bethel Harper. And *maybe,* maybe that's why it happened."

45

"But what happened?"

Her sharp eyes narrowed. "They didn't tell you about Bethel Harper, and how he took himself out the other night and went up on the ridge, and fell from it to the rocks below?"

"I didn't know," I gasped. "I knew there was a funeral yesterday, and that's why Rory Calvert met me, but I didn't know . . ."

"Didn't you now? Well, I'm not surprised. What's the good of hashing it over for you? *You* didn't know him. And there was enough talk in town as it was. Oh, they got him buried fast, just twenty-four hours after the inquest. And nobody there but them. No flowers. No nothing. They put him in the ground off by himself, and that's the end of him. So now you're here."

I couldn't stop my gaze from moving from her face to the gaping hole where the window had been. She must have easily followed it, and just as easily read my thought.

"Another accident last night, wasn't there?" she said, rather than asked. "One more small thing." She limped a step closer to me. "If you were smart you'd decide you don't want to be company here. You'd get yourself away from this place, Teena Halliday."

"But why? What do you mean?"

Her pursed mouth spread in a crooked smile. "So many accidents, Teena Halliday. If you don't believe me ask in town. Go to Tumlee and see what the people say about Rentlow Retreat."

"But I don't understand," I told her.

She glanced toward the open doorway. Then turned back to me. "You're just a child," she whispered. "Just a child." Then, "Bethel Harper lasted here a week, and death comes by threes, so how long do you think you can stay?" Voice raised, as if she hadn't been whispering before, she went on, "Yes, and you ought to see Tumlee. It's a sweet town, and a friendly one. For some, that is." She turned from me abruptly. "The family's gathering for breakfast. It's time and past time that we both went in."

46

I apologized for the delay I caused, and went inside with her, my mind busy with what she had told me.

The Rentlows had said only that a friend of the family had died, not mentioning that he'd been staying with them, that a fatal accident had killed him.

There had been so much talk about me in the week before I'd arrived that Mrs. Foxall had thought that I might not come.

And more important than anything else, Mrs. Foxall had warned me to leave Rentlow Retreat.

Why?

There had been so many accidents, she said, and that reminded me of what happened the night before. Death comes in threes, she said. And Bethel Harper had died.

The family sat in the breakfast room. Sunlight was bright on the table, cheerful anenomes in a blue dish at its center. The smell of strong coffee was good, normal.

I took my place. It was hard, in that morning atmosphere, to take Mrs. Foxall seriously. I told myself that she must be, like Maria, a superstitious country woman, and perhaps like Maria, too, in being sometimes put out by having her work increased by guests.

Jeremy rose to greet me, his smile warm and compelling. "Good morning, Teena, love. Are you recovered from the awful shocks and alarms of last night?"

"Of course I am." But even as I spoke, I wondered who had taken away the broken window frame. I wondered how I could find it again. More than ever I wanted to look at it by daylight. Had I just imagined that the bar was sawn through? I went on, "After that, I slept like a log."

Aunt June's washed-out blue eyes seemed to search my face. "I'm sorry, Teena, dear. But this is such an old house, and I suppose that with that terrible wind ... if only it hadn't been your room ... if only ..."

Uncle Charles cut in, "Yes, it was the wind. But no harm's done."

I thought that the wind would have blown the glass in, not out. But I didn't say anything.

Uncle Charles went on, his glasses glinting at me. "And it will be repaired by this afternoon. I found the frame

47

this morning, and took it right to the ironsmith in town. He'll bring it back and install it as early as he can."

Now I knew who had taken the window frame away, and I knew, too, that I would never be able to make myself certain of what had happened.

I would never know if someone had stood in the shadows of the terrace and called my name in a whisper, or if it had been a dream.

Mrs. Foxall served breakfast quickly and silently. When she refilled my cup, she bent close to me. Her sharp black eyes met mine.

I thought of her warning, and remembering that Jeremy had promised to take Scuffy into Tumlee to see a veterinarian, I decided to go with him. I didn't know what I would discover there, but if I could find the ironmonger in time I might examine the window frame, and if I could talk to someone in town I might understand more of what Mrs. Foxall's hints meant. If they meant anything.

I said, "Scuffy's not down this morning, is he? When are you going to take him to Tumlee, Jeremy? I'd like to go along for the ride."

He bent his dark head. "There's no use to it now."

"But Rory said . . ."

"Poor little Scuffy must have died sometime during the night," Jeremy went on.

Uncle Charles put down his cup. It made a sharp crack of sound in the sudden silence.

I said slowly, "I'm very sorry. I didn't think . . ."

"I'm going to bury him this morning," Jeremy told me.

I nodded.

"It's what I always do," he went on. "And I even have his gravestone ready." His dark eyes suddenly glittered at me. "Of course I didn't intend it to be his gravestone. But I was doing him in marble. And I finished last night. Just before . . . So you see . . ."

Aunt June cut in, her voice shaking, "All right, Jeremy, that's enough."

And Estrella said, "It's so beautiful today, Teena, I thought it's a perfect day for showing you all around the grounds. We have some interesting things for you to see, and the view from the ridge is . . ."

Jeremy rose. "I'll want company, Estrella. You and Teena must come with me. I don't care to have funerals alone."

Uncle Charles muttered a warning, "Jeremy, listen to me . . ."

But Estrella said, "All right, Jeremy. All right. We'll come down to the grove with you."

CHAPTER FIVE

We walked together under the thick leafy elms. The clear air was thickening, growing heavy with moisture, but the sun was still bright on the smooth green of the lawn where Jeremy's statues stood frozen in perpetual poses.

Jeremy carried the smooth, unweathered figure of Scuffy, posed as he must have sat, head down on small white paws, eyes dreaming dog dreams.

Estrella held in her arms the wooden box into which Jeremy had put Scuffy's thin body. Her sultry mouth was grim, saying, "You ought to have outgrown this a long time ago, Jeremy."

"Outgrown sentiment?" he asked. "How foolish if you thought I would, Estrella."

"I could hope, couldn't I?" she asked bitterly.

And I wondered what excuse I could find for asking Jeremy to drive me into Tumlee.

We reached the lawn. I saw that Jeremy had already prepared a place. There was a narrow deep hole. Beside it lay a shovel.

Estrella silently put the wooden box into the grave. Jeremy adjusted it to his satisfaction, then covered it over with a mound of soil. At last he carefully set in place the small stone figure of Scuffy.

I remembered how he had circled away from Jeremy to go to Rory, how he had leaned against my ankles. I had realized that the dog was ill, but somehow I hadn't thought that he would die.

There was something odd, even frightening, about those moments.

I remembered how Tony had buried a cat for me when I was a tiny child, and how once, together, we had found a mangled bird, and carefully made it a respectable grave. Children did such things as a matter of course. It was part of life, Tony had always said.

But here, surrounded by statues—fawns, owls, dogs, cats—and remembering how they had seemed to move through the curtain of rain the evening before, I felt a sense of terror.

The very silence was oppressive. There was not a single bird call. No dog barked. Even the leaves on the great oak along the lane were utterly still.

At last, Estrella said, "That's enough, Jeremy. Let's go."

But he turned to me. "All my pets, you understand. They're all here. This is my private cemetery."

"Jeremy!" Estrella, turning her back on us, flung her dark hair from her face. "That's enough, I say. Don't be so morbid."

He grinned at me. "Sisters aren't very patient, nor very understanding." He put a warm slim hand under my arm and looked into my face. "But you, Teena, you understand, don't you? So come on. Let me show you around."

I allowed him to lead me from statue to statue. Unwillingly, and with a peculiar pounding of my heart, I listened while he told me about each of them, and how he had sculpted them, and how the models had died and been buried.

Estrella waited at the edge of the lawn, her slim body ridged with tension. Beyond her, I saw Mrs. Foxall peering from the front window, then from the partly opened doorway.

Jeremy's soft voice went on, low, husky, hypnotically gentle, giving me the names, even the biographies, of the pets he had buried there.

And then, suddenly smiling, he said, "I hope you don't think that I'm showing off, Teena, love. I just wanted you to have a good look. As a homage to what

50

I've loved, I suppose. And to see if you think all this a fitting memorial."

I felt a sudden cold. The silence around us had become painful. But I said, "Of course it is, Jeremy. You do beautiful work."

"You haven't really seen it yet," he told me. "But you will now." He led me back to where Estrella was waiting. "We're going to have a look at the maze now," he told her.

"Oh, Jeremy, not now," she protested. "I want . . ."

"But how long will it take? Really, Estrella, you can be so difficult."

"It's just that I wanted . . ."

"First the maze," he said firmly. "I want Teena to see the figures there."

"I know that," she flared. "But, oh, all right, if you insist."

He grinned suddenly, "And afterward I thought we might drive over and visit Rory."

"Now that's a wonderful idea," she exclaimed, all opposition to Jeremy suddenly abandoned.

We went down the lane toward the high hedges that walled the maze. At its entrance there was a single marble fountain.

Jeremy bent over it, and with a whispering ripple water spewed upward in a bright spray from the mouth of a fish. "I did this too," he said, leading the way between the thick wall of hedges.

Within them, the air was heavier still, the silence even more oppressive. I followed him slowly, wishing he had not brought me there.

The path twisted, turned, doubled back on itself. I was hopelessly lost almost immediately. I was very glad I wasn't alone.

Jeremy turned a corner, disappeared for a moment. When I caught up with him, he was standing beneath the statue of a tall slender woman. "One of my first efforts," he said, smiling at me. "How do you like her?"

"She's beautiful," I said.

Estrella murmured, "Let's go on."

51

"I was fifteen when I did her," Jeremy went on, his dark eyes glinting at mine.

"Who is she?" I asked.

"Her name was May Argon. She used to work for us."

"Come on," Estrella cut in. "If we delay too long, Rory might go out."

Jeremy shrugged, went on. He seemed to have decided that Estrella's impatience had reached the breaking point. He led me past several other figures, both human and animal, and suddenly, when I had begun to think that there was no end to the maze, that I would be trapped within it forever with him and Estrella, he suddenly stepped out into bright sunlight. Beyond us there rose a great outcropping of gray stone that rose against the blue of the sky.

I turned to look back, and Estrella grinned at me. "You can't see it from this end."

I knew instantly what she meant. The exit from the maze seemed to have disappeared as we left it. There was a great tangle of wild rhododendron, drooping with thick glossy leaves, overgrowing the tall hedges.

I took a deep breath, glad to be out in the sun again.

"We can shortcut to Rory's from here," Estrella said.

"Oh, not yet," Jeremy answered. "We'll drive over later. I want to show Teena my studio first."

"But you said . . ."

He grinned at her. "If you refuse me my small pleasures, then I'm going to refuse you yours, Estrella."

She gave him a sulky look, but didn't answer.

I was relieved that the tug of war was over.

But I was as disappointed in the delay as Estrella was. I was anxious to see Rory Calvert, anxious to talk to him. I had promised to tell him if anything troubled me. And already I felt as if I had so many things to report to him. So many questions to ask.

But Jeremy led us back to the house.

I saw Mrs. Foxall watching us approach. Moments later, we passed her in the hallway. Her eyes met mine, then fell away.

Jeremy took me up to the third floor. Estrella trailed us, still sulking and silent. As Jeremy opened the door

52

to his studio, I heard Mrs. Foxall limping up the steps.

Jeremy crossed through cool shadows to throw back heavy dark drapes while I waited on the threshold with Estrella.

Sunlight flooded the big room. I drew my breath in, dazzled by the whiteness of wall, by the glow of marble, by a spaciousness that seemed alive with quick movement, though in fact, there was very little that was movable in that room.

Around the white walls, there were stacked blocks of stone of all shapes and sizes and textures. A huge dark table dominated the center area. On it lay a litter of tools, mallets and chisels, drawing pencils, scraps of paper, sketch pads.

A narrow couch, covered in a rough dark fabric, stood by itself. Nearby there was a straight wooden chair.

Jeremy nodded at it. "Sit down if you like, Teena. See what it feels like."

Estrella, still on the threshold, said, "Oh, no, you're not going to stall us here, Jeremy Rentlow. I know your tricks. Hurry up and show Teena around and get it over with."

"You're in such a rush," he mocked her, grinning at me. "My poor sister, all she can think of is Rory Calvert."

"Oh, stop it." she shrugged impatiently. "Teena's seen the studio, now let's go."

"The gallery," he said softly.

She bit her lip. "Jeremy, why do you have to be so stubborn? Teena's going to be here for a long, long time. She can see the gallery . . ."

"Rory's going to be there for a long, long time too," he grinned.

He took my arm and led me to a door I hadn't noticed earlier. It was odd that I hadn't seen it at once. It was painted a sharp shiny black, and stood out from the wall that surrounded it.

He opened the black door, stepped inside, momentarily lost in the gloom. Then a brilliant light suddenly glowed, and he beckoned me inside.

53

I took two steps, and stood next to him, looking around the windowless room.

We were surrounded by figures, figures of all shapes and sizes, in all positions of movement and repose. They were beautiful things, glowing, sleek, almost alive. They were of every subject imaginable. Animals, birds, people— oh, yes, more people than anything else.

It was an indoor replica of the animal cemetery on the lawn outside. And, strangely, it gave me the same odd feeling of discomfort.

Estrella stood at the threshold, her hands twisted together, her face strained and pale. "Oh, come on," she said.

Jeremy's dark eyes were on me, waiting for my re- action, I knew. Waiting with too much intentness for my reaction, I felt.

I found it hard to summon enthusiasm, to compliment him with proper awe.

At last, I said slowly, "These are beautiful, Jeremy. So very beautiful. They seem almost alive to me."

"I loved them all," he told me softly.

Estrella made a protesting sound.

Jeremy turned his head, regarded her silently for a moment, then looked back at me. "I did, Teena," he said. "A piece of my heart is within everything I've ever done in stone. It started when I was in my teens, and it's never stopped. It never will." He paused. Then, with a gentle smile, he went on, "And one of these days soon, Teena, love, you'll sit in that chair, and look at me just as you're looking at me now, wearing that white dress you wore when you came last night, and I'll cap- ture you in marble, in the whitest, purest marble I've ever used. I'll capture you forever."

His dark eyes held mine. His soft gentle voice seemed to linger in the air.

I felt an odd melting within, and a peculiar hunger to reach out, to touch him suddenly.

Estrella's, "Oh, Jeremy, no, no, no," was soft as a bird wing moving through the still air.

After a moment, Jeremy moved away from me. He went to a mahogany stand, put his fingers on the slim

bare shoulder of a girl. His hand moved in a light strok-
ing movement, a fondling gesture, a caress of the cold
stone, that somehow signified regret. He smiled, looking
back at me.

The girl had long flowing hair, smooth along the shape
of her tilted back head. Her empty eyes seemed to
regard the high white ceiling with hungry passion. Her
cheekbones were high, round. Her throat was long and
arched.

I studied her for a moment, while Jeremy's hand
caressed her lovingly, and his dark smile held me silent.

I knew her. I had seen her before. I had seen a
picture of her on Estrella's dresser. The girl Jeremy had
done in stone was Sarah Calvert, Rory's younger sister.

Jeremy let his hand drop. He turned to me with a
rueful glance. "Sorry. I forgot for a moment."

"Let's go," Estrella cried.

"Yes," he agreed, and took my arm.

It seemed to me that his fingers caressed my flesh
just as they had caressed Sarah Calvert's cold hard
shoulder.

A shiver went through me.

CHAPTER SIX

I was glad when we left the gallery and studio behind us.

Jeremy's figures gave me a sense of unease, and more
than I wanted to admit to myself, I was aware of a
peculiar feeling that I had toward him. A feeling of
attraction that was, at the same time, laced with re-
pulsion.

I told myself impatiently that I mustn't let my
thoughts be diverted by imaginary sensations and intui-
tions. I had real problems to think about.

What had happened to Ben? Why hadn't he met me?
Where would I find him?

Had the incident with the window the night before
merely been an odd accident? Or had it been an attack
planned on me?

Why had Rory Calvert told me that things were not

always what they seemed, and warned me to be on my guard in Rentlow Retreat?

Why had Mrs. Foxall told me to leave?

The hallway outside Jeremy's gallery and studio was filled with the scent of lemon oil. Once again I felt a wave of homesickness. Lemon oil reminded me of Maria. But it wasn't Maria wielding the cloth on the desk in the alcove that led to the attic. It was Mrs. Foxall. She jerked her head at us as we went by, and I felt her sharp eyes follow me as I went down the steps with Jeremy and Estrella.

Estrella hurried out to the terrace, then around the side of the house to the garages, plainly eager to be on her way to Rory's.

But Jeremy said, "I have to go back. I forgot the gate. It'll only be a moment."

I stood in front of the garage, looking into the shadows. There were three cars there, and as I looked them over, Estrella said, "Come on, we'll have time to walk back down to the sea."

She led me past the garages to the back of the house, through a strand of low trees, then a narrow strip of brush. Way off to the left, I saw the rhododendrons that marked the place where, earlier, we had emerged from the maze, and the stone ridge against the sky. As we neared the ridge I saw that it was made up of huge gray boulders. We climbed up, Estrella surefooted as a cat, I following more carefully. From the top, I could see the ocean far below us. I had time for only a quick look at the waves boiling in to the rocky shore.

Then Jeremy called us, and we hurried back to him.

We drove down the rutted lane under the tall arching trees. The statuary on the smooth lawn was still and white in the hot sun. I turned my eyes quickly away from it, not wanting to think of the new grave in what I now thought of as Jeremy's cemetery.

Jeremy stopped to open the gate, and I found myself holding my breath, wondering if it would really be unlocked, if I would really soon drive away from Rentlow Retreat.

The few hours since my arrival the evening before

seemed to have stretched out endlessly. So much had happened. And yet, when I thought about it, it seemed that not much had happened at all.

But the tall gates did open, and as Jeremy drove through, they closed again behind us.

Estrella said, "I hope Rory's home."

"He will be," Jeremy retorted. "And just waiting for a proper time to turn up, the way he always does."

"We're all he has left," Estrella said quickly. She went on, "I'm sure you'll understand if I ask you not to mention Sarah's death to him. He's still terribly torn up about it. They were very close. We all were."

The car rocked and skidded as Jeremy raced it around the curved road, and spun it right, and went speeding on.

I wished he would slow down, and I knew that Estrella, biting her lip, with her dark eyes averted, was wishing the same.

Finally she said, "Jeremy, I'm sorry. I didn't mean to upset you. But I *did* think we ought to warn Teena." She took a deep breath, her dark eyes on his somber face. "You know how he is. And . . ."

Jeremy turned and gave me a quick look. "I'm sorrier than Estrella is. It's just that sometimes, when I remember how it was . . ."

I nodded, pretending to understand. But he knew I didn't. He went on, "You see, Teena, Sarah and I were engaged. And when she died, I lost . . . I lost more than I could bear losing."

I thought of the figure he had done of her, of the others. All of them had a piece of his heart in them, he had said.

Estrella flung her hair back. "Poor Teena, you're really getting the full treatment, aren't you? When you arrived you found us in mourning for Bethel. And then there was that awful business with the window. And now, here we are, burdening you with our gloom about Sarah." She turned toward her brother. "Really, Jeremy, I think our family's too much. The least we could do is not load Teena with our private mourning."

He gave me a smile, and my throat was suddenly

tight with sympathy. It must have been terrible for him to have loved Sarah, and then lost her, lost her in her beautiful youth, before their shared dreams could come true.

He slowed at a bright red mailbox, turned right. We rolled along an arching driveway lined with tall white birches. Beyond them I saw a low white house, bright with blue shutters, surrounded by huge shiny rhododendrons.

"Rory's," Estrella said, a lilt in her voice.

Jeremy parked, and the three of us got out.

Rory came to meet us.

Estrella ran ahead, caught his arm, swung him around. "Isn't it a lovely day, Rory? Oh, it's so good to be out and away."

Quick laughter followed her words and seemed to me to add, "And to be away from home." It was an echo of the way I felt myself.

I looked at Rory's auburn head, and tall, lean figure, dressed in blue slacks and a matching blue shirt, and asked myself if my relief, so strong as to be a tangible thing, was at seeing him again, or simply at having escaped from Rentlow Retreat for a little while.

Jeremy slid a too-possessive arm around my shoulders, smiled. "My sister wears her heart on her sleeve, wouldn't you say?" he murmured.

Plainly Estrella did, and didn't care, nor try to conceal it. I found myself wondering, though, if her demonstrativeness could be for my benefit. Was she warning me that Rory was her personal property, and off bounds as far as I was concerned?

Rory gave her what appeared to be a rather brotherly hug, and led us to a side porch, which was filled with plants, window boxes of bright petunias, giant pots of ferns and palms, urns of fragrant snapdragons. The furniture was white wrought iron, soft with blue cushions. It was a peaceful and beautiful place, and I instantly responded to it. It somehow reminded me, in atmosphere, at least, of the patio at home.

I looked around, enjoying the atmosphere, but wondering at the same time how I would manage to talk to Rory alone.

"And he does it all himself," Estrella said proudly. "Can you imagine? Our Rory has a green thumb and four green fingers besides."

"I celebrate life," he said softly.

There was a small significant silence. I couldn't understand what he had said to provoke it. Then Estrella cried, "Rory, you can't imagine what happened last night. The wind blew out one of the casements in Teena's room and scared all of us out of our wits."

Rory's dark brows drew together in a frown that seemed to sharpen his dark green gaze. "The wind, Teena? What's this?"

Estrella didn't know how I had dangled in the dark, clung to the draperies with all my strength, head down in the night, before I dragged myself back to the safety of my room.

More than ever I wished I could find a chance to speak to him alone, to tell him what had happened. I wanted to tell him that I thought I heard someone calling me, and believed it to be my father. I wanted to tell him that it seemed to me the window had simply fallen away when I touched it. I wanted to ask him why Mrs. Foxall had warned me to leave, just as he had warned me to be on my guard. And I wanted to ask him to take me in to Tumlee. I suppose I hoped he would lay my growing fears at rest, reassure me and relax me.

But he said expressionlessly, "What an odd thing to happen."

"Wasn't it?" Jeremy agreed. He sprawled in a love seat, patted the place beside him. "Come sit down, Teena."

I took a chair nearby.

"You weren't hurt, Teena? Nothing like that?" Rory asked.

"Oh, no," Estrella cried. "Of course not. It's nothing. I wouldn't even have mentioned it, except that it scared us so."

"What did the vet have to say about Scuffy?" Rory asked after a moment.

Jeremy sighed. "It was too late. He died during the night, Rory."

"He died?"

"We buried him this morning," Jeremy said stiffly.

Rory nodded, said he would get us iced tea and cookies, and went into the house. Estrella followed him, insisting that she would help him.

Jeremy said thoughtfully, "You're very quiet, Teena. Are you always?"

I told him I supposed I usually was.

"Do you think you'll like being with us?"

I lied as boldly as I could, assuring him that I knew I would like it. But my words rang emptily in my ears. I hurried on, saying, "Except that I'm so anxious about my father."

"Of course you are. Since you seem to have expected him." Jeremy paused. Then, "But I just don't see . . ." He allowed his voice to die. "Are you sure it wasn't someone's idea of a joke, Teena, love?"

"But that would be quite impossible."

"Then I really don't understand. You see, Teena, love, it's just as my parents told you last night. We've had no contact with your father for years. I don't even know how many." He shrugged. "There was something, I suppose. These things do happen in families."

I didn't tell Jeremy, but I supposed that the "something" he referred to was Uncle Charles' anger that Margaretha had chosen Ben to marry instead of him, and possibly his further discovery, on his marriage to Aunt June, that neither of the sisters were as wealthy as he assumed. And that once Margaretha and Ben were divorced, Uncle Charles had cut them both out of his life. I asked myself then why, if that were so, had he agreed to have me come to stay with him.

Jeremy's dark eyes were fixed on me. "You've missed your father all these years, haven't you? Missed him terribly."

"I've wanted to see him." I answered carefully, hoping to avoid any disloyalty to Margaretha.

"Still," Jeremy said softly, "You'd do better to forget him, Teena. I know what it's like to lose someone loved.

60

But I know, too, that there comes a time when it is necessary to forget the past and look ahead only to the future."

His words hung between us; his dark eyes watched me with warmth and sympathy. I couldn't help but respond to his kindness, yet I knew that he didn't really understand. It was more necessary now than it had ever been for me to find Ben. If my suspicions were fact rather than sick imaginings I was in danger in Rentlow Retreat.

As meaningless and far-fetched and unbelievable as it seemed to me, danger was a possibility I couldn't deny.

Rory and Estrella returned, bringing the refreshments.

After a while she grew restless. She rose, wandered about the sun porch. Finally she asked Rory, "Why don't we climb down to the sea?"

He agreed and rose.

I waited for Estrella to ask me to go along, but she didn't. Somehow I didn't want to be alone with Jeremy then. I didn't want to sit in the fragrant scent of the flowers, and face his somber eyes.

It was Rory, saying, "Come along, you two," who gave me the excuse I wanted.

I immediately got up, saying, "I'd like to see what the ocean looks like here."

"It's different from what you're used to," Rory told me.

He went ahead, leading the way, with Estrella right on his heels, and Jeremy striding along beside me.

We crossed a narrow back lawn, then stepped into a grove of stunted and wind-sculptured trees and waist-high but thin brush. Moments later, we left the grove behind us. The damp earth under foot gave way to stone, small shale, and then boulders, beyond which I saw nothing but the blue of the sky.

Rory picked a path for us to a rim of rock, and paused there waving us on. When I reached the rim, I stared down breathlessly. Far below, wind-lashed breakers slapped endlessly on the jagged black teeth of upthrust boulders, and swirled in great sucking pools between them. I shivered in the warm breeze.

"Let's go down," Rory said, and turned away, leading us step by step along an unmarked trail that rambled between shelves of stone, through narrow openings, past dark-filled caves.

Somehow though I didn't quite know how he managed it, he dropped back, was at my side. Estrella and Jeremy were far below us, dark heads lowered, concentrating on the descent.

"Are you all right?" Rory asked quickly, softly.

I nodded.

"What happened last night?"

"Just what Estrella told you. Except that I . . . well, I wondered if it were really an accident."

"Why?"

I told him about the voice I thought I'd heard calling me, how easily the window frame had given way, how, if I hadn't caught the velvet drapes, I would have fallen to the terrace.

"I have to talk to you," he said soberly. "I'll fix it. Follow my lead."

I nodded. I saw, past his wide shoulder, that Jeremy had stopped, was turned back, watching us.

We climbed down to the shore. I was surprised to find a calm and beautiful cove, formed by an elbow of rock that curved out from the bottom of the cliff. On the side on which we stood, there was soft glittery white sand, and small quiet ripples. Beyond the elbow of rock, the sea boiled up, frothing and dangerous. The ridge above us was dark gray. A single upthrust boulder leaned dangerously into the air.

Somehow it didn't surprise me to learn that Rory's land ended at that curving arm of stone that reached into the sea, and that beyond it, stormy and frightening, Rentlow property began.

Jeremy saw me glance up, once, twice, then again, at the single boulder that seemed to reach for the sky. "That's Retreat Point," he said.

Rory and Estrella were silent.

"It's frightening-looking," I said finally.

The others were still until Rory said, "We'd better get back."

The climb up was slow, breathtaking. I was relieved when we reached the blue-shuttered house. And that was when Rory said, "Oh, listen, Teena, I have business in Tumlee. Why don't you ride along with me so that you can have a look at our great metropolis? I'll bring you back when I'm through."

I immediately agreed, knowing that this was his means of giving us an opportunity to speak together alone.

Estrella looked from me to Rory, said petulantly, "I can't imagine what you think Teena needs to see in Tumlee."

Rory grinned at her. "Just because you don't think much of the town, doesn't mean that Teena won't enjoy it as a tourist."

"Think much of it?" Her sultry mouth twisted. "Ugh! I hate Tumlee, and you know it."

Jeremy laughed softly. "Estrella's so sensitive."

Estrella flung back her dark hair, cried, "Oh, never mind! Go ahead, you two, but Rory, you must promise to come for dinner."

"I'd planned to invite myself," Rory retorted.

Jeremy urged Estrella into his car, gave me a thoughtful look, then a small wave, and drove away.

"I have no business in Tumlee," Rory said, when we were alone.

"But I do, Rory."

He gave me a long steady look, then led me to his car. "You can tell me why you do, and in that tone of voice, on the way," he said.

We drove by the red mailbox. I looked at it, then I wondered why there was no mailbox before Rentlow Retreat. I asked Rory.

"They don't deliver to the Rentlows," he told me.

"Why?"

He shrugged. "There are so many 'whys,' Teena."

"It's just one more thing, isn't it?"

He glanced at me. Then, "What do you mean?"

I drew a deep breath, not quite knowing how to begin, not knowing how far I could trust Rory. Finally I said, "Yesterday, just a little while after you met me, you asked me to think of you as a friend, to tell you if I felt troubled by anything, or worried, in Rentlow Retreat."

He nodded. "And now . . .?"

63

"There are so many things, Rory." I heard the quiver in my voice and paused, struggling to compose myself. "I felt as if you were warning me," I went on finally. "Then last night . . . I realize it could have been a crazy accident. But, just the same . . ."

"You think it might not have been?"

I nodded. "And then, this morning, Mrs. Foxall told me about Bethel Harper, and how he fell from the ridge. It was . . . it was from Retreat Point, wasn't it, Rory?"

"Yes. None of us mentioned it because . . . well, because these things are unpleasant. The less spoken of the better."

"I know that. But when Mrs. Foxall told me about it, she told me to go away from Rentlow Retreat. She was warning me too, Rory. But I don't know about what."

"Mrs. Foxall . . ." he said slowly. "I see . . ." Then, "Did she mention May Argon to you?"

For a moment I was stumped. I knew the name but I didn't know how I knew it. Then I remembered the slender figure in the maze. "The girl that Jeremy sculptured," I said. "No. Mrs. Foxall didn't mention her to me."

"But that's what she was thinking of when she talked of Bethel Harper's death. May Argon was her younger sister, Teena. May Argon worked for the Rentlows about ten years ago. I remember her very well, of course."

"She *was* Mrs. Foxall's younger sister," I said tonelessly. "What happened to her?"

Rory hesitated, then, "She threw herself off Retreat Point, Teena."

A shiver went over me. My breath froze in my lungs. I whispered, "And Mrs. Foxall took her place, working for the Rentlows then?"

"Oh, no, she's only been with the Rentlows for about six months. It was after my sister"—his big hands were white-knuckled on the steering wheel as he finished the sentence—"my sister died." He drew a long slow breath, then said very quietly, "Teena, I think you must go away. You must go now, today, and go as far as you can."

CHAPTER SEVEN

His heavy words hung between us, ugly with a meaning I couldn't understand.

At last I breathed a single word. "Why?"

"I don't know," he said firmly. And then, green eyes giving me a quick narrow glance, said, "Not that I want you to go, Teena. You must know better than that. But that I think you must."

"You still haven't told me why."

"Too much has happened. That's all I can say."

All he could say? I asked myself. Or all he would say? Did he have reasons of his own for wanting me gone from Rentlow Retreat? Or was his concern for me real?

I thought of my terror the night before, the unease that had dogged me ever since I saw the Rentlows waiting for me on the terrace of the big stone house. And then I thought of the cable from my father. I said, "Rory, I can't leave until I hear from Ben. He knows I'm here. He knows where to reach me. If I should leave . . ."

"He'd find you. If he looked," Rory said.

Moments later we drove into Tumlee. It was a small village. Its single paved street led from a post office flying a bright flag at one end to a white-steepled church at the other.

"You've still not told me why you wanted to come to town," Rory said, as he parked and cut the car motor.

"Mrs. Foxall. She told me if I wanted to know about Rentlow Retreat I should come to Tumlee.'

Rory sighed. "Teena, I should have explained more. Ever since her younger sister died, Mrs. Foxall has been . . . well, let's call it a bit distraught. You can't go by what she says. She's . . ."

But I was only half-listening. Further along the block I had seen a drugstore. I peered forward to study the sign above it. Finally sure, I said, "That's Foxall's Drugstore, isn't it, Rory?"

"Yes. He's her husband."

"They don't do well?"

"What do you mean, Teena?"

"The drugstore doesn't make a living?"

"What? Oh, no, it does very well indeed. I handle the accounts."

"Then why does Mrs. Foxall work at Rentlow Retreat? From what you've just told me, they don't need the money she makes there."

Rory's face was suddenly hard as sand stone. Hard ridges appeared around his lips, worked in his jaw. He said softly, "Teena, what are you getting at?"

"I don't know. But it means something, doesn't it? She's afraid of the place. She always leaves before dark. She told me so. Yet she works there. Why? She started working there about six months ago. Just after your sister died. Why, Rory?"

He pursed his lips in a silent whistle, but he didn't answer me.

"What's happened between when May Argon died and your sister died?"

He shook his head.

"Why did Mrs. Foxall come to Rentlow when she did?" Again he shook his head.

"Rory, why did Mrs. Foxall say Tumlee was the place to find out about Rentlow Retreat?"

He smiled faintly. "That's easy. Small towns talk. Tumlee talks. About Rentlow Retreat."

"And what do the people in Tumlee say?"

He shrugged, got out of the car. He opened the door on my side, drew me out with him. "Teena, small town gossip means nothing."

"But enough so that Estrella hates the town, and doesn't want to come to it."

"Doesn't want to?"

"Otherwise she'd have insisted on joining us," I told him. "And you knew that when you suggested it, Rory."

"All right," he said. "That's true."

But when I asked him what the gossip was about he merely shook his head, asked, "Well, where do you want to go?"

"Can we find the place where Uncle Charles would have brought the window to be repaired?"

Rory nodded, led me down the street to a hardware store. He introduced me to Mr. Prouty, a tiny man, gray-haired, and soft-voiced, who said, "Mr. Rentlow brought the window in, and I fixed it, and I've just come back from installing it. So what do you want here now?"

"I wondered how it was broken," I told Mr. Prouty.

"Ask in Rentlow Retreat," he retorted, and turned away from me.

"That wasn't much help, was it?" Rory said, when we were outside.

I didn't answer.

"And now?"

I didn't know what to say. I had the feeling that as long as Rory was with me no one would talk to me. Or perhaps it was because he was known to be friendly with the Rentlows.

"We might as well go back," I finally said unwillingly but unable to make a substitute suggestion.

On the way back to the car I noticed a small white clapboard building. Rory must have seen me glance at the Public Library sign on its door.

"Want some books?" he asked. "You can borrow on my card if you like. Until you get your own. If you stay long enough to bother with that."

I decided that I liked the idea of having some books to read. It was one of my favorite occupations. I followed Rory inside.

He introduced me to a plump, middle-aged woman, whose purple hair was teased into what looked like a shaky leaning tower of Pisa. "This is Teena Halliday," he said. "She'd like to borrow on my card, Mrs. Bagley."

"Teena Halliday?" Mrs. Bagley repeated, small blue eyes peering at me worriedly. "Now where have I heard that name?" She smiled at me. "No matter, child. You're welcome here. Just take what you please."

I heard her light voice chatting with Rory as I wandered from shelf to shelf, choosing a book here and there. With three that seemed interesting I returned to the desk.

As she stamped the back flaps of the books, I said, "I'm staying at Rentlow Retreat, if you want to write down my address."

"Rentlow Retreat," she breathed, the stamp falling from her plump hand to the floor. She stepped back as far as she could from the counter. "Then what do you want here?"

"Teena's Mrs. Rentlow's niece," Rory said quickly. "She's on a brief visit."

"Brief visit, is it? Poor child," Mrs. Bagley answered. "Let's hope so. Let's hope she doesn't find herself here forever."

"Mrs. Bagley," Rory cut in quickly.

She gave him a quick pale glance. "Sorry, Rory. I was forgetting for a moment. But there *was* poor May, wasn't there? And your own sister Sarah? And the Harper man that never left."

The blood left Rory's face, leaving greenish pallor under his heavy tan.

Still standing as far from me as she could, Mrs. Bagley pointed a plump finger at the wall behind me. "You might be interested in that subject," she whispered. "It might help you, though it helped no others."

Rory's hand curled around my shoulder, urged me toward the door. I allowed him to lead the way, resisting only long enough to glimpse the section head on the case Mrs. Bagley had indicated. In neat black letters it said: *WEREWOLVES, VAMPIRES, and SUCCUBI.*

"But what did she mean?" I asked as Rory took me to the car. "What was she talking about?"

"Just what Mrs. Foxall said you would hear in Tumlee," Rory said grimly, and drove me back to Rentlow Retreat. He dropped me off, promising to return later.

Estrella was in the foyer when I went in. I wondered if she had been lingering there, waiting for me, for Rory.

She wanted to know, "Was it fun? Did you see our great big city from one end of Main Street to the other?" Without waiting for a reply, she slipped the books from under my arm. "Oh, you visited our gorgeous library? And how is dear Mrs. Bagley, that madwoman?"

"Madwoman?" I asked.

"Half the people in Tumlee are mad," Estrella said, laughing. She gave the books a cursory glance, then thrust them at me. "What happened to Rory?"

"He said he'll be back later on in the day."

She leaned against the wall, half-blocking me. I didn't know if that was an accident or design, but I couldn't quite nerve myself to brush past her.

"Rory's quite taken with you," she said softly.

"He is? I think he's very nice."

"He must be. Else why would he bother?"

"Bother?"

"To take you to Tumlee. Just because you wanted to go."

"He said he had an errand," I reminded her, for that's what he'd said earlier.

But she laughed at me. "What errand?"

"He wanted . . ."

She shook her head so hard that her long black hair veiled her face momentarily, then swung away uncovering it again. "Teena, don't, please don't. It doesn't matter. I've known Rory all my life. Do you think I don't know when he's lying to me?" Her dark eyes swept my face. "I suppose I should have warned you, explained to you, Teena. I wouldn't want you to get yourself hurt. We're first cousins, and kin should be kind to each other. And we're the same age just about, so I know how you feel, and I know what it can lead to."

"I'm not sure I know what you mean," I told her.

But I was sure. Even before she spoke I knew what she was going to say.

"Rory Calvert. That's what I mean," she said gently. "I suppose he sees that very faint resemblance of yours to Sarah. And that's why he keeps falling all over you. But that's all it is. So you mustn't get any ideas. Rory is mine, Teena. We've loved each other for as long as I can remember. I don't intend to lose him to you, or to anyone else."

I said stiffly, "And I've known him just twenty-four hours. I don't think this discussion is necessary."

"If you're your mother's daughter, and I'm certain that you are, then time has nothing to do with it. I just

69

want to be certain that you clearly understand. Rory Calvert is off bounds for you."

I didn't answer her. I brushed past her, started for the steps. I blinked back tears, carefully putting one foot ahead of the other, clutching the polished bannister as hard as I could.

Mrs. Foxall was standing, empty-handed, on the second floor landing.

I wondered how much she had heard, what she was thinking. She didn't speak to me, and I didn't speak to her.

I was halfway to the third floor when I heard Estrella call out, come running behind me. She caught up with me, flung an arm around my shoulders. "Oh, Teena," she cried. "I'm sorry. I don't know what's the matter with me." She giggled, hurried on, "Oh, yes, I do too. It's the green-eyed monster. Please forgive me. We never go anywhere, nor meet new people. Rory's all we have. All I have. But you and I aren't going to fight over him or anything else."

I found myself laughing with her, relieved and glad, my tears forgotten.

Still hugging me, she went with me to my room, saying, "I trust you all the way, Teena. And I trust Rory too. He's always been so good, so kind to everyone. But sometimes I just . . ." She flung herself on my bed. "I think it's because I miss Sarah so much. We all do. And even though he doesn't speak of it Rory does more than the rest of us, of course. In a way, at least. It was so awful. The way it happened. And she was so young. So alive. We needed her, you see. We really needed her to make our foursome right."

I set the books carefully on the white mantel over the fireplace. The huge gold-framed mirror reflected my face, and at my back, Estrella's.

She said, speaking to my reflection, "We've none of us really gotten over it. Not Rory, not me, not Jeremy."

"What happened?"

"Poor Sarah . . . poor Jeremy . . . it was soon after they became engaged. Some blood thing. Anyway, she just gradually faded away. You couldn't notice it in the

70

beginning, but pretty soon she was no more than a pale white skin and frail bones. There was nothing anyone could do. Within a few months it was all over. Jeremy was desolate."

"The head of Sarah that Jeremy did," I said thoughtfully. "The one in the gallery. When did he do that, Estrella?"

"What do you mean?" she demanded, a curiously flat note in her voice.

"I wondered if he had worked from memory. Or from pictures. Or just what."

Estrella swung her feet to the floor and rose. She stretched hugely. "I might as well get dressed. Maybe Rory will be back soon." She went to the door, then paused. "I might as well tell you. If I don't, someone else surely will. Jeremy was working on Sarah's head when she became ill. He finished it the day she died."

Estrella wore white. Her hair was piled high in a shining crest of curls. Long glittery earrings brushed her cheeks. She insisted that I join her on the terrace to watch the sunset. I was sure that actually she was watching for Rory to come as he'd promised.

Mrs. Foxall stamped out of the house, banged the heavy door shut behind her.

When I told her good night, she paused and looked at me. "Good night to you, Teena. As for me, it will be. As long as I'm gone before dark."

Estrella chuckled as Mrs. Foxall limped away down the lane. "Isn't she a dream. Rather a nightmare, I should say. Do you know her husband won't even come in and get her?"

I didn't answer. I watched as Mrs. Foxall made a wide circle, getting as far away as she could from the fountain at the entrance to the hedge maze. Something about it reminded me of Scuffy, making a wide circle around Jeremy to go to Rory.

"A real character," Estrella went on. "The area's just full of them."

I made a sound of acknowledgment, thinking of Mrs. Bagley in the town library, and her plump hand pointing

71

at the shelves marked Werewolves, Vampires, and Succubi.

Rory drove up then, and Estrella rushed to meet him. Moments later, Jeremy joined us.

Dinner was more pleasant that night than it had been the evening before, even though Uncle Charles was as grim as ever, and Aunt June was haggard and edgy.

Rory and Jeremy kept the conversation going between them.

I found myself comparing the two of them. Rory, so strong-looking, steady, and safe, and self-contained, his green eyes narrowed watchfully, it seemed to me. And Jeremy, so handsome with his dark curly hair and intense black eyes that more and more often met mine.

After we'd eaten, June and Estrella and I cleared the table. June and Charles disappeared upstairs.

Jeremy and Rory and Estrella and I played cards for several hours. When, at last, Rory rose to leave, he said, "I'll have a look at your window, Teena. Just to make sure Mr. Prouty did a proper job of installing it."

I protested that it seemed quite all right, but he insisted.

We all went up together, Rory leading us, in a way that was completely natural. I took a peculiar pleasure in the thought.

Jeremy and Estrella watched silently as he drew aside the green drapes that had been re-hung, and opened and closed the window several times.

I went to the mantel. The books I had left there had been shifted so close to its edge that they seemed about to tumble to the floor.

"It looks all right now," Rory was saying, as I reached out to move the books back.

I half-turned to answer him, and at the same time, the wall above me seemed to come slamming down, to explode with a great roar, and I found myself spun off my feet and in his arms. I was caught up in the swiftness of his lunging dive, rolled away and flung aside.

I lay in his arms, his body half over mine, his cheek against my hair. I felt the pounding of my heart, and of his too. Beyond his shoulder, I saw the faded place on

72

the wall over the fireplace. I saw the big square which the huge mirror had covered until moments before.

I was hardly aware of Estrella's shrill scream, or of Jeremy's barely audible curse.

Rory moved cautiously and drew me with him.

Around us glittering in thick shards lay what remained of the mirror. One piece was streaked moistly with red.

Rory lifted me to my feet, sat me in a chair. Dazed, shocked, not quite understanding, I sat still, while he told Estrella to get ice, ordered Jeremy to phone for a doctor. It was only when he ripped off a pillow case, folded it and pressed it to my shoulder, that I realized I had been injured, that I at last felt pain.

He leaned close to me, whispered, "Do you believe me? You must leave here, Teena," and before I could answer, he was across the room, his footsteps crunching in the shattered mirror, searching the floor around the mantel, then the mantel itself.

"I don't know," he murmured, as if to himself. "I don't see anything. But still . . . still . . ."—and then he looked toward me—"Teena, there's something wicked happening here. You must promise me you'll go."

There were hurrying footsteps on the stairs.

I closed my eyes. Rory, I knew, held the same suspicions I did. How could that heavy mirror have fallen by accident? How could there have been one accident the night before, then another one tonight?

If Rory hadn't been there, if I'd come into my room alone, and gone to the mantel, I would have died beneath the slashing crushing weight.

I was sure now that the danger in Rentlow Retreat was real. But I didn't know the motive behind it, nor the force that moved it. I knew only that it existed.

"Dear God," Aunt June wailed. "What shall we do? What's going to happen next?"

Eyes still closed, breath frozen with fear, I silently asked myself the same question.

CHAPTER EIGHT

"Remember what I told you, June. Remember. I mean what I say." Uncle Charles' voice was a cold, grim whisper.

Aunt June wailed, "There must be something we can do."

I opened my eyes to bright sunlight. The first thing my gaze encountered was the bare spot over the fireplace. I looked away hastily. I didn't want to remember, but those frightening moments the night before came flooding back in swift jagged recollections, painful as the shards that had cut into my shoulder.

I remember that Jeremy had given a muted cry, and stared at me, his face white, his thin lips drawn back. And that Estrella had screamed. But mostly I remembered Rory's arms around me, lifting me, carrying me to the chair, his voice a deep whisper. "Something wicked is happening. You must leave." And then Aunt June's anguished wail. "Oh, dear God, what's going to happen next?"

In what had seemed to be only a few minutes, Dr. Paul Benson bent over me. He was tall, thin. He had white hair, and a lined face, both thoughtful and non-revealing. He sent everyone from the room, and worked over me quickly, making small wordless sounds of reassurance that painfully reminded me of Tony's crooning as he picked sand spurs from my feet when I was a child.

It was only when he was finished, the long narrow cut stitched together, and painted and bandaged, that he sat back, asked, "How did this come about?"

I didn't quite know how to answer him. What purpose would be served by making accusations I couldn't prove? I said finally, "The mirror fell. I suppose something loosened it, and then . . ."

"There's talk in town that a window casement broke out last night," he said gently.

"Yes," I agreed.

He studied me. I had the uncomfortable feeling that he

might be able to read my mind. I closed my eyes against his too penetrating gaze.

"Are you planning a long visit?" he asked finally.

"For about six months."

"Why?"

"The Rentlows are the only family I have." I went on to explain about Margaretha. It seemed perfectly natural for him to question me, and me to answer. He was that kind of man.

He listened, nodding, and plucked at his lip. Then he gave me a pill, saying it would help me sleep through the night.

Aunt June came in, wringing her hands and demanding tearfully, "How is she, Dr. Benson?"

"No serious harm done." He rose, snapped his bag shut. "I've given her a tranquilizer. And I'll leave two more. For tomorrow, just in case. I'll want her to come in a day after tomorrow for a check of the stitches. One can't be too careful."

Aunt June thanked him with meaningful intensity.

He stared at her for a moment, then smiled gently. "My dear June, you seem more upset by this than Teena herself. I think perhaps I should leave something for you to take too."

She protested, but he gave her several pills, ordered her to take them, and left.

Aunt June fussed around me, twitching the sheet over my bandaged shoulder as if she couldn't bear to look at it. "I've worried about that mirror," she murmured. "But, you know, Teena, somehow, one never thinks such a thing could happen. Why, it's hung there for so long, and not a crack to be seen . . . who would believe . . ."

"Did Rory go?" I asked.

"He's still downstairs, Teena. But you must sleep now."

"I'd like . . ."

"No, child," she said firmly. She closed the drapes over the window, then stooped to peer down at me. Her pale blue eyes suddenly filled with tears again. "Rest well, Teena," she said. Then, turning out the light, she left me.

Silence, thick, heavy, and ominous, enfolded me. There

was not a whisper of sound anywhere. There was not a footstep, a breath.

The pill Dr. Benson had given me seemed to have set me afloat on soft dark clouds. I told myself dreamily that I must leave Rentlow Retreat. I reminded myself that I must wait for my father to come to me. When Ben came, then I would be safe. And finally, with that thought still in mind, I drifted away into uneasy sleep.

But now the sun was shining.

I had heard Uncle Charles and Aunt June whispering just outside my door. I listened as they walked away, and then I sat up. I found my green robe and put it on. My arm was stiff, but my shoulder didn't hurt until I sat at the dressing table and tried to brush my hair. It was then that quick hot waves of pain swept me, leaving me chilled, shivering. I dropped the brush and waited breathlessly for the chill to subside. Soon I could breathe again, move again.

I managed to dress, moving cautiously. I had just put my slippers on when Mrs. Foxall came in, carrying a breakfast tray.

More than ever her face looked shrunken and yellow as she gave me a disapproving look. "I'm told you're to stay abed today."

"I'm all right," I told her. "Except that maybe my arm is a bit stiff."

She put the tray on the bedside table, then went back to the door. She opened it, turned her head, plainly looking up and down the hall. Then she closed the door firmly and came limping back to me.

She sat down, folded her hands in her lap. "It could have been worse," she said.

I nodded.

"You remember that I told you death comes in threes."

I nodded again.

"Well?"

I waited for her to go on.

She said softly, "You're braver than some, and maybe you're stronger than some, but that won't save you."

I looked into her eyes, asked carefully, "Mrs. Foxall,

76

are you thinking about your sister May? Do you suppose that what happened to me last night—"

"And the night before," Mrs. Foxall cut in.

"—do you think there's a connection to your poor sister's death?"

Mrs. Foxall gave me a confused look. "Do I know? How could I know? Ten years ago almost she died. And before then"—Mrs. Foxall made a whimpering sound in her throat—"before she threw herself off Retreat Point . . . how she talked in the nights, and with me listening too; wild, wild, it was, Teena."

"And Bethel Harper, Mrs. Foxall? Did he talk wild too?"

"I don't know about him. Just that he was always laughing, and then they said that he . . ." She got to her feet. "Don't blame me for what happens. I've told you. Remember that I've told you."

But I was still thinking of Bethel Harper. I asked, "Where did he come from?"

"I don't know."

"But who was he?"

"I don't know that either. And I don't ask too many questions."

"Then you'll never know the answers, will you?" Jeremy asked, grinning from the open doorway. He gave Mrs. Foxall a narrow-eyed look. "Don't you have things to do downstairs?"

She limped from the room, hurrying faster than her poor legs could take her.

Jeremy stood beside me, his dark eyes rueful. "I'm afraid I scared her away. But she is such a bore, and she talks so much nonsense. I try to be patient but there are times when she's more of a trial than I can bear. This is one of them. I want to look at you, quietly, and without her babble as background. I want to reassure myself that you're all right."

"I am, Jeremy." And I thought as I said it, Thanks to Rory.

"I knew you'd be. Nothing can hurt you here. I wouldn't let it." His voice was very soft, deep. His slim fingers cupped my cheek. I found myself unable to move.

His hand held me, his look held me. An invisible web seemed to have gathered around my body.

Then he smiled faintly. "I'm going into my studio to work for a while. I'll be back later on."

Rory and Estrella were in the living room when I finally went downstairs.

"Estrella said you were still sleeping," Rory said, getting to his feet.

"That's what I thought," she said defensively.

"Are you okay?" Rory asked me.

I nodded.

"I'll take you into Tumlee to see Dr. Benson the first thing tomorrow morning," Rory said.

"I can do that," Estrella protested.

"My pleasure," Rory told her absently, giving me a significant look.

Estrella curled her long legs under her. "You're accident-prone, aren't you, Teena? So many accidents in such a short time. I doubt Rentlow Retreat's good for you. I think you'd do well to find yourself another nest."

"That's what I've been telling her," Rory agreed.

"And what's that?" Uncle Charles demanded, his wide shoulders blocking the doorway. His hard flushed face swung enquiringly from Rory to Estrella. "What's this you're saying?"

Estrella was silent.

Rory answered, "Teena has been thinking of leaving."

Uncle Charles' rimless glasses glinted at me. "She's free to go, as she pleases, of course. It is totally up to her. And to her alone. But it was Margaretha's idea that Teena come here, and I don't know what Margaretha would say if Teena were to leave."

I knew what Margaretha would say. But that wasn't what held me in Rentlow Retreat.

I said, "I have no plans to leave, Uncle Charles. I really don't. Rory and Estrella were just talking."

"I see," Charles said.

I went on, "But I do want to reach my father. And if you could think of some way . . . if you knew . . ."

Charles turned in the doorway. "I think you'd do well to forget him."

"But . . ."

"I know. The cable." Charles smiled faintly. "You're a stubborn, single-minded child, aren't you? It was all some odd mistake. Ben Halliday couldn't have known you were coming here. Unless your mother told him. And that, I'm quite certain, is very improbable."

When her father had gone, Estrella muttered, "I just don't understand you, Teena."

Rory said tiredly, "Teena, you must listen to me," but stopped as Jeremy joined us.

Estrella, I knew, was thoroughly jealous of me, fearful that Rory's interest in me might grow. No wonder she wanted me gone from Rentlow Retreat. But did she really consider me such a threat that she could have tampered with the window, the mirror, in hopes that I would be frightened away?

Rory had told me I was in danger when I first came, repeated it yesterday, then again last night. Was he so certain that what had happened had not been two accidents? Or did he have some other reason for wanting me to go? Or, in his grief at losing his sister Sarah so suddenly, did he imagine dangers that didn't actually exist?

Jeremy's smile warmed me. He said gently, "Don't listen to them, Teena." I noticed that even as he talked to me he gave Estrella a swift hard glance.

She seemed suddenly still.

Rory looked speculatively from her to Jeremy.

Jeremy said, "I want you here, Teena. I wouldn't let you go."

Rory made a small wordless sound of protest.

But Estrella cried, "Jeremy!"

He ignored her, said, "Of course I want you here, Teena. You already know that. And we must start in my studio this afternoon. That's what I've been doing. Getting all ready for you. And later on, we'll . . ."

Again Estrella cried, "No!"

Rory cut in. "Teena should rest. After what happened last night . . ."

"Nonsense. What she needs is diversion. And I propose to see that she gets it from now on." He turned his

79

back on Rory. "You do want to pose for me, don't you, Teena? You do want to see yourself grow in marble."

I thought of Sarah, her tilted head flung back and her empty eyes. I thought of May Argon standing slim and tall, frozen forever in the terrifying maze. I thought of Scuffy, head on his paws, crouching in Jeremy's animal cemetery on the sloping green lawn.

I promised myself that I would never never sit for him. I didn't know then how soon he would change my mind.

I said only, "I'm not a fit subject, Jeremy. I'd rather not let you try it."

"But you will, you know," he answered gently.

"Jeremy, you can't," Estrella cried. She came and stood close beside me. I could hear her breathing hard. "Really, Jeremy, you mustn't."

"Why not? When I have no other subjects now? And Teena is so beautiful. Why not, Estrella? Or would you prefer to model for me yourself?"

Rory, white-faced, grim, interposed, "Jeremy, you're not being fair to Teena."

But Jeremy grinned. "Shall we let her make her own decisions? She's old enough to say yes or no."

I smiled at him, then said gently, "Then it's no, Jeremy."

"We'll see," he answered.

Rory said lightly, "Stick to your guns, Teena." As he excused himself and went home, all warmth and ease seemed to go with him. I felt so alone that I wished he had taken me back to his blue-shuttered house.

Soon after, Uncle Charles asked Estrella to join him in his study. Jeremy said he would go up to his studio to work, and disappeared.

I went outdoors, then around the house and down the path to the ridge. I stood there, staring at the sea below.

It was dark that day, oily, sluggishly pulsing against the coast line of rocks in slow whirlpools. Beyond the long curved elbow of boulders that reached out from the shore, I saw a small figure on the Calvert property.

I thought of the children I had watched play on the beach below the villa. They had had sharp snapping

80

brown eyes and sweet easy laughter. My longing for home was unbearably intense.

I sought, and finally found, a narrow path that cut down the cliff face. I went carefully around the huge projecting boulder called Retreat Point, and made my way down to the rocks below. I climbed over them into a sunlight that seemed brighter, onto sand that was soft and white. I knew I had left Rentlow Retreat behind, and come to Rory Calvert's land.

For a little while I stood in the shadow of a big gray boulder, watching the young boy I had seen from the ridge. He had seemed much smaller from that distance, and younger. Now I could see that he was thirteen or fourteen, a wiry towhead, wearing blue jeans and high boots, and busily intent on wading out into the shallow ripples and casting a line as far as he could.

He seemed unaware of me until a sudden gust of wind caught his line just as he flung it out and whipped it back at him in a great loop. He spun around, reaching for it. But when he saw me, he stopped.

I raised my hand in greeting, but he didn't respond. Instead he grabbed up his line and began to bundle it every which way into a knotted ball.

I went to him, stumbling in the sand. "I didn't mean to chase you away," I said.

His blue eyes flashed up at me. The freckles seemed to stand out on his face. "Did you come from there?" he asked, jerking his head at Retreat Point.

"From a path behind it," I said, and went on, "I'm visiting the Rentlows."

"I don't go over on that side. Rory Calvert lets me come down here, but here's where I stay. This is as close as I go. I promised my folks."

I nodded. "Then that's what you have to do."

"It's what I *want* to do. I don't like it over there."

"Why not?"

"Do you?"

"It's all right."

He suddenly squatted down on his heels. "Didn't you ever notice that nothing lives there? Birds don't nest around Rentlow Retreat, and dogs and cats don't go

81

there, and there's not a fawn in the hills that doesn't go miles around to keep away."

"But why?" I asked.

He shrugged. "It's a dead place, like they say in town." He looked up at me. "I don't know why you'd want to stay there."

"I'm waiting for my father," I told him.

"Oh." He was still for a moment, then he rubbed his hand on his jeans, and stuck it out. "I'm Jimmie Hunnicut. You don't know that, of course. But I know who you are. You're Teena Halliday." He went on, explaining, "Everybody in town knows that too."

I shook his hand and said formally, "I'm glad to meet you, Jimmie."

He nodded, then tipped his towhead back and stared up at Retreat Point. "That's a bad place, Teena. You be careful when you're up there. It's a killing rock. It got May Argon a long, long time ago, and it got that man last week, and I think it got Rory's sister Sarah, too."

"Sarah? But she was sick, Jimmie. She died of a blood disease."

"Maybe. Maybe not. And I'm not the only one that thinks maybe not. Plenty of folks in town keep talking about it. And Mrs. Foxall, she purely loved Sarah Calvert too, and they say that's why she works out there now. To find out what happened. To May. And to Sarah."

"I expect that's just gossip, Jimmie," I said, but I knew that I was hearing the truth. I'd wondered myself why Mrs. Foxall had come to work at Rentlow Retreat when it had sad memories for her. I'd wondered why she'd taken a housekeeping job when her husband's drugstore could surely support the family. Young Jimmie Hunnicut had given me the answer.

I looked up at Retreat Point, shuddering suddenly.

It was death-cursed, and claimed its victims one by one. May Argon. Sarah Calvert. Bethel Harper. I wondered who would be next.

Jimmie raised his hand in a farewell gesture. "I hope your father comes soon," he said.

"Now sit here, Teena, just as I place you," Jeremy said. He moved me, his hands firm on my hips, then shifting to my shoulders. His fingers brushed the bandage, and I winced. He apologized quickly, and moved me again, as if I were a rag doll without wit or will. "Just so, Teena love. Does the light hurt your eyes?"

I had promised myself that Jeremy would never do a statue of me, yet here I sat in his studio, avoiding his brilliant glance. I didn't quite know how it had happened, except that moments before, as I was on my way back to my room, he had waylaid me.

"Now's when we start, my Teena," he'd said. "I can't wait any longer." He drew me with him. I protested as politely as I could, but plainly not strongly enough to persuade him that I meant it.

He led me into the studio and switched on the overhead lamps that threw brilliance on the white walls and high ceilings.

He patted the block of marble on the table, grinned at me over it. "Just relax, Teena. It won't hurt. It won't hurt even a tiny bit."

Mrs. Foxall limped through the open door. "I was going to do a clean-up in here," she said indignantly.

Jeremy narrowed his eyes at her. "Now?"

"Right now."

"We're busy," he told her.

"She ought to be in bed, resting up, getting over that last night business," Mrs. Foxall said.

"I'm going to amuse her into forgetting all about it." Jeremy went to the door, holding it open. "Please?" he smiled.

She gave me a long look, then went out.

Closing the door firmly, Jeremy went back to the table and leaned on it. "Not that way, Teena love," he said softly. "Please, not that way. You're all stiffened up. Relax, and dream . . ."

His soft voice went on and on, lulling and gentle, murmuring compliments, and promises, and endearments.

I watched the swift neat movements of his long hands, and listened to the sound of his voice rather than the words he spoke, and finally, after what seemed a long time, I heard him ask, "Teena, are you tired? You've been such a good girl. Do you want to stop now and stretch, and have a good rest before dinner?"

CHAPTER NINE

I came to myself with a sudden start, aware of a pinprick of pain at my throat. Within moments it faded away and I completely forgot about it, just as I soon forgot the strange tiredness I felt for a little while.

Jeremy was saying, "You see? It's not nearly as bad as you thought. Teena love, why didn't you want me to?"

"I don't know, Jeremy."

That was true. I didn't know. But it had something to do with Sarah and May and little Scuffy. It had something to do with what young Jimmie Hunnicut had pointed out to me: that no birds sang in Rentlow Retreat, and no dogs or cats wandered there. It was a feeling. And I knew it to be irrational, but just the same I promised myself that I had done my first and last sitting for Jeremy.

I discovered in the following weeks that my promise was more easily made than kept. But I didn't know that the day Jeremy began his work.

The following morning Estrella drove me in to see Dr. Benson. He checked the stitches in my shoulder, said they were doing nicely, and told me to come back the next week. When Estrella and I were finished, I suggested that we take a walk around Tumlee, but she insisted that we return immediately to Rentlow Retreat without offering a reason for her hurry. I supposed that she hoped Rory would drop in and didn't want to miss seeing him. Her hope proved to have substance. Rory was waiting for us on the terrace.

"What did the doctor say?" he asked me.

"She's just fine," Estrella answered before I could speak.

"When do you go back, Teena?"

"Next week," Estrella told him.

His green eyes narrowed. "Teena?"

"Next week," I repeated.

Estrella frowned at his implied rebuke, and frowned even harder when he said that he would be away for a few days, visiting clients around the state. Soon after, he left us, and Jeremy came out to ask if I were ready for another session.

Estrella protested crossly, "Oh, why don't you leave her alone?"

"Substitute for her today?" Jeremy asked sweetly.

"That'll be the day," Estrella retorted, and went inside.

"Ready?" Jeremy asked me.

"I'd rather not. Not today," I told him.

He came very close to me, put a gentle hand under my chin and tipped my face up. He stared into my eyes. "Teena love, please, please."

I felt the depth of his attractiveness, the compelling need to respond to him. I thought no, and found myself saying yes.

It was two weeks later.

I was in Jeremy's studio, the glittering white walls aglow with late afternoon sun.

I was thinking that soon I must suggest that we stop. There was something that I had planned to do for several days. What it was, at the moment, escaped me. I tried to concentrate. I knew it was important that I remember.

Time had passed in an odd blurring way. I had seen Dr. Benson three times. On the last visit he had removed the stitches and said I needn't return. Each time Estrella had driven me into Tumlee and hurried me back again.

There had been no more threatening accidents, and the night when I clung so desperately to the velvet drapes seemed long, long ago. The evening the mirror fell from over the mantel, and Rory held me in his arms, seemed never to have happened. Except that I had never forgotten the sense of safety I had felt at his touch, and never had it again. I began to believe that my suspicions had been wild imaginings, that I had seized on a pair of coincidences out of my unwillingness to stay in Rentlow Retreat. As for Rory, he traveled quite a bit, he told us. When he was home, he came over each day. It seemed to me that he watched me carefully, but somehow I never saw him alone. Estrella jealously made sure of that, and Jeremy, more and more possessive of me, abetted her, I was certain. More than that, though, I sensed that Rory and I were not the friends we had started out to be. He had disapproved of my sitting for Jeremy, and told me so bluntly, and I felt that he thought less of me for doing it. Whenever I let myself think of him, I felt a great aching loneliness that neither Jeremy's smile, nor Aunt June's continual fussing over me, could make me forget.

I still hoped my father would come, but I found myself thinking of him less and less often, just as I wondered only occasionally now why I had still not heard from Margaretha.

But now I sat in the studio, and Jeremy murmured softly. I couldn't quite hear the words. It seemed to me that whenever I sat for him, almost every day in the past two weeks, I had somehow lost track of time and found myself mindlessly drifting, unoccupied and unstirred. I suppose it came from the silence around us, from the whiteness of the walls, the shiny black of the closed door to the gallery where Sarah Calvert stood mutely staring at the ceiling forever. I supposed the absolute motionlessness that Jeremy insisted I maintain had a soporific effect.

Somewhere below, a door slammed. I gave a start of surprise. What I had been trying so hard to remember was suddenly clear. I wanted to ride to Tumlee with Mrs. Foxall.

Jeremy asked, "What is it, Teena?"

"If we could stop now . . .." I said finally, able at last to form the words that so oddly had seemed to tremble on my tongue against some barrier that held them.

"Are you in a hurry?"

"No, but I thought . . ."

"Poor Teena. You hate this, don't you?"

86

"Oh, no," I protested quickly. "I find it interesting, Jeremy."

"You do?" He smiled at me. "I'm pleased. You know, when we began you had to be persuaded so. I felt I was pushing you against your will. But it was for your own good. You seemed so lonely, at loose ends. I didn't want you to be."

I got to my feet, leaned against the chair. I ached all over. My legs were stiff. My arms felt numb. Even my throat seemed vaguely sore. And I was so tired. I realized that I always felt unaccountably tired now. I imagined it was because I was losing weight. My clothes had become a size too large, and I'd taken to pinning my waistbands with safety pins.

I reminded myself that I had no time to waste. Not if I wanted to catch Mrs. Foxall. She was punctual to the minute, and I knew nothing on earth could delay her into staying in Rentlow Retreat after sundown.

Jeremy was saying, "You mustn't be lonely here. You have me."

"I'm not, Jeremy." Then I went on, "But I'd better hurry, if I'm going to catch Mrs. Foxall. I want to ride into town with her."

"You needn't do that. I'll drive you in. Just give me a moment's notice, and I'll be glad to. Any time . . ."

I wished I hadn't spoken. I couldn't remember that Jeremy had been to Tumlee since my arrival, and I didn't want to go with him anyway. I simply wanted to be away from him, from all Rentlows for a little while.

But plainly Jeremy was determined to be kind to me, as he had been since we first met, trying to amuse and divert and make me feel at home.

He said softly, "Teena, don't you realize what has been happening? Are you really so terribly young and inexperienced that you haven't been able to read what's in my mind and heart?"

I waited, not sure of what he was about to tell me, but hoping it wasn't what I feared. I had seen the warmth of his look, noticed how often he touched me, sensed a growing depth of feeling in him. And I had found myself responding to him more and more, unwillingly aware of his attractiveness. But we were first cousins, and I knew that any emotional relationship between us must be confined to the boundaries of kinship. Yet Jeremy's eyes offered more that cousinly affection.

Now he said, "You *do* know, Teena."

I moved shakily away from the chair, wondering at my exhaustion. It hardly seemed reasonable that I should feel so depleted, just from sitting for three hours. I said, "I'll go down now, Jeremy. We're cousins. We oughtn't to talk like this."

He was very still. He seemed taller, his body in shadow looking up like a slim monument to forgotten gods. His face was suddenly unreadable, the same shadow hiding his features.

"You feel the same as I do," he said finally.

I stopped at the door and leaned there, bracing myself against a peculiar dizziness. "Jeremy, we're first cousins."

He came toward me, smiling. Oddly he seemed to leave the shadow behind him. "That's all that bothers you?"

"It's a fact."

"Is it?" He took my arm. "Teena, we're not related by blood."

"What do you mean?" I gasped.

"The Rentlows adopted me when I was an infant. I'm their child by law, but not by blood. So you see . . . what you call a barrier is no barrier at all."

I was hardly able to believe what he'd said. I was frightened, repelled, without knowing why. I didn't know how to answer him.

He seemed to understand. He touched my cheek gently. "Never mind. Just remember."

I went downstairs, trying to hurry, but somehow finding it difficult to move one foot before the other, to force speed into coordination. Just as I reached the foyer, the door slammed. I went to it and opened it. Mrs. Foxall was hurrying down the driveway, limping as rapidly as she could in a wide circle around the white fountain that marked the entrance to the maze.

I called to her, but she didn't seem to hear me, and

at the same time, Jeremy said, "Never mind, I'll drive you in myself, and then you can be sure of a ride back, which you wouldn't have been if you went with the Foxalls."

"I needn't bother you," I protested. "I just thought I'd return my library books and get new ones."

"We can do it now." He turned away. "I'll be back in a minute."

He returned, dangling car keys, whistling softly. "I've set the release for the gate. All ready?"

I nodded.

His eyes narrowed on my face. "But, Teena, if you want to return your books, hadn't you better take them with you?"

I looked down at my empty hands. My cheeks burned with a swift blush, and a peculiar fear swept me. I seemed so incapable of thinking, remembering. I glanced up the stairs. My room was three flights up. The thought of that climb was terrifyingly difficult. I wondered what was wrong with me. How could I be so tired, so limp, drained?

Jeremy said, "I'll get your books. Sit here and wait."

I sank down gratefully. He touched my hair, then ran up the steps. Moments later he was back.

We walked together around the house to the garages. As Jeremy backed his car out, turned it in the driveway, I noticed again the third car that was parked in the shadows. I had seen no one drive it. Not ever. I wondered why.

Jeremy saw me glance at it and said, when I joined him on the front seat of his car, "Americans are automobile crazy, as you've probably guessed by now."

I laughed, but I wondered why its back plate was different from the ones on the other two cars.

We covered the few miles to Tumlee in only a few minutes, yet I knew if I tried to walk it it would take me a very long time.

Jeremy parked the car before the library and got out with me.

"I won't be long. If you want to wait here . . ."

But he came inside with me. Mrs. Bagley looked up when we entered the big quiet room. Her leaning tower of Pisa was the same, but her hands froze on the card she held, and there was no welcome in her face when she saw us.

Jeremy wished her good afternoon. She jerked her head, her lips moved without a sound.

I sensed chill cold fear, projected without word or movement. It wrapped itself around me, icy bonds that seemed to hurt my flesh.

Jeremy gave me an affectionate push. "Go on, Teena, see if there's anything you want."

I set the books I was returning on the counter. I saw Mrs. Bagley's eyes move from Jeremy, from Jeremy and me, to the bookcase behind us. I turned, saw the small classification notice. Werewolves, Vampires, Succubi.

I asked, "Anything you recommend, Mrs. Bagley?"

She whispered, "Nothing," and averted her eyes from those shelves.

I wanted to take a book from that category, just because she had directed my attention to it and aroused my curiosity, but somehow, her manner decided me. I'd do that another time—when Jeremy wasn't watching me so intently. Instead I quickly chose three books of poetry, hardly attending to their titles, and Mrs. Bagley checked them out, not asking me for a card, but assuming that I would still use Rory's. I told her I'd like a card of my own. She handed me the forms. I filled them out, signed them. She checked them, put them aside, said, "You may pick up your card when you come in next."

I thanked her and said, "Then I'll see you soon."

She didn't answer me.

Outside, Jeremy laughed, "She's a sour old biddy."

But I wondered.

Jeremy suggested that we stop in Foxall's Drugstore for a soda. I agreed, though I'd just as soon we went back to Rentlow Retreat.

He said, "You remember the figure in the maze? May Argon? The girl who used to be housekeeper for us? Did you know she was Mrs. Foxall's younger sister?" I nodded, and he went on, "Poor May. I always liked her. The way a fifteen-year-old does, you know. But she wasn't quite . . . well, I don't know how to say it exactly. She just wasn't very bright, I suppose. Young, pretty as a picture, as I remember her, but somehow... perhaps retarded is the word, or perhaps it was a matter of confusion. The trouble we had when she worked for us... you wouldn't imagine. Still, because she was as she was, and it couldn't be considered her fault, we did put up with it. But then..." He sighed. "Poor May."

Jimmie Hunnicut was stacking newspapers outside of Foxall's. He glanced up at me, recognition in his face.

I grinned at him, but he shot Jeremy a glance, and his face became blank. He stared through Jeremy, through me, and turned and walked away before I could speak.

Jeremy seemed not to have noticed. I didn't say anything, but I knew now why Jeremy didn't come often to Tumlee. He wasn't welcome there. I wondered why.

I wondered, too, why I hadn't told him that I knew about May Argon, and why Mrs. Foxall worked at Rentlow Retreat.

May and Sarah had died, and Mrs. Foxall had loved them both. It seemed a long time since I had thought of that. Too long.

Inside Foxall's, Jeremy and I sat at a tiny table and sipped the sodas Mr. Foxall had served us without greeting or comment.

Hoping to have some conversation with him, I introduced myself.

His eyes peered at me from twin nests of deep wrinkles. "I know," he said, his voice so rusty that I wondered when he had last used it. Then he backed away to stand behind the soda fountain.

Jeremy and I finished our sodas, and he paid Mr. Foxall, and the two of us left, Jeremy saying, "You don't understand, Teena, the way things are in these poor towns. They are so backward, even dying, with the young going away, the old remaining with no means to make a living. They resent anyone who has money. They hate us, you see, for our two cars, and our estates. They hate us because they envy us."

It was only when we were driving back to Rentlow Retreat, thinking over what Jeremy had told me, that I remembered what he had said about owning two cars.

Two cars, I thought. Not three. But there were three cars in the garage. I almost remarked on that, but managed to stop myself in time. Three cars. I kept thinking about it. It seemed important. I didn't know why.

We stopped at the high iron gates. Jeremy got out, and moments later, with the release pressed, he returned and we went through. He drove around the house, into the garage.

I glanced toward the third car, pulled way over into the shadows. I looked away hastily, without understanding my sudden uneasiness.

But Jeremy had noticed. He said, "Oh, that was Bethel Harper's. We haven't disposed of it yet."

I stood very still. There had been something in Jeremy's tone, in the way he said the name, that struck me. For the first time I realized that Bethel Harper had the same initials as my father. Bethel Harper. Ben Halliday. I had never thought of that before.

I wondered if that, too, was simply an odd coincidence, but I decided to find out as much as I could about Bethel Harper. I knew only that he was a family friend of the Rentlows. He had visited them for a week before his accidental death. But what had he looked like? How old had he been? Where had he come from? Could he have been my father, Ben Halliday, but using a different name for some reason?

Jeremy put his arm around my shoulder, drew me with him back to the house. "Never be bashful to ask me to take you to Tumlee, Teena, or anything else, I'll do what you want. Do you understand? That's how it will be from now on."

I thanked him, leaned against him. Tiredness swept over me. It was good to be needed, wanted, loved, good to be pampered and cared for. For a little while I forgot my questions.

But later, when I was alone, I remembered Bethel Harper, and the car in the garage, and I made up my mind that somehow I would find out the truth.

Rory joined us for dinner that night.

Estrella sat beside him, glowing, her dark eyes fixed

on his face, her slender hands reaching out to touch him, to attract his attention whenever it wandered for even a moment.

We had just finished eating. Jeremy excused himself, then returned carrying a bottle of champagne. He opened it, then said, smiling at me, "I have something to tell all of you." He filled my glass, then the others. He raised his glass to mine. "Drink to Teena, everybody, and drink to me. And then wish us luck."

I heard Rory's breath draw in sharply. I looked from him to Jeremy, bewildered and unsuspecting.

Jeremy said joyfully, triumphantly, "Teena has promised to be my wife."

CHAPTER TEN

I heard the words, but somehow I couldn't believe that I had heard them right. Jeremy had never asked me to marry him. I had never consented. He had, in the past weeks, made it more and more clear that he loved me, and I had been more and more drawn to him. But I still felt a peculiar and disturbing sense of being repelled by him. It came and went at odd moments. I couldn't explain it, but it was real.

In the sudden silence that fell at Jeremy's words, someone gasped, a shoe scraped. I gathered my strength at last and said, "But Jeremy . . . Jeremy, I never told you . . ."

At the same time, Rory shoved back his chair. "Teena . . ." He spoke my name gently, but with reproach.

I had promised him not to commit myself to anyone or anything. I hadn't really understood what he meant then. But now I realized that this, just this eventuality, was what he must have had in mind. It had occurred to him the moment he saw me at the airport. I wondered why.

Now Jeremy was smiling ruefully, "Please, Rory. I know how you must feel, what you're thinking and remembering. I should have realized that you . . ."

He was referring to Sarah Calvert, I realized. He was saying that Rory must be remembering Sarah and how she had died a slow, sad death. That must be why Rory was staring at me with green eyes narrowed. That was why his face was so pale that it seemed bleached and bloodless, and his mouth was twisted with bitterness. Rory was remembering Sarah, and thinking that she, not I, should be Jeremy's bride.

The recognition was bewilderingly painful. It left me dazed, unsure of myself, and speechless when I should have spoken.

Estrella leaned forward to touch Rory gently. Her voice soft and sweet, she said, "Rory, dear, we all understand. But you must realize that life goes on. And surely you've seen what was happening between Jeremy and Teena. Why, from the first moment they saw each other, when you drove her up, and she got out of the car . . ."

She glowed, beamed, smoldered. Triumph was hot in her shining dark eyes. I had always known she was jealous of me, but until that moment, I had never realized the depth of her fear that Rory was interested in me. But I had no time to ponder the meaning of that.

Rory, his eyes still on my face, said, "Of course. I understand." He seemed to relax, his big hands going still on the table edge.

Finally I managed to say, "Jeremy is a little premature anyway. We never really . . ."

Uncle Charles' cool voice broke in, "We're all delighted, my dear. And we do understand your . . . let's say your caution. After all, you two young people have known each other for so little time. Still . . . love doesn't take long, eh?" He gave a quick hard laugh. I realized it was the first time I had ever heard him laugh. I decided that I didn't much care for the sound of it. Jocularity was oddly out of place for him.

Aunt June said briskly, "We're all pleased." But her words were peculiarly hesitant when she went on. "And you might begin your toast again, I do think."

Jeremy lifted his glass. "To Teena."

The others echoed him.

I heard no sound from Rory.

The others drank. I watched and saw that he didn't.

"You must drink," Jeremy told me.

I raised my glass, sipped. The champagne was cold, tart, slightly sickening. It burned my lips, my throat.

Rory rose. "If you'll excuse me . . ."

Estrella stood up with him, pouting prettily. "Why, Rory," she laughed, but with no joy, "how can you be such a dog in the manger? If I didn't know better, I'd think you wanted Teena for yourself!"

My heart gave a swift sudden leap, thudded painfully against my ribs. Rory . . .

He gave Estrella a blank look, and then walked out of the room.

Estrella sighed, "Well, I guess it's our fault. We ought to have prepared him for it. And I oughtn't to have teased him." She gave me a hard stare. "I hope you and Jeremy will be very happy," she told me, and tossed her glass into the fireplace. It shattered with a loud sound that reminded me unpleasantly of the mirror exploding in my bedroom weeks before.

It was so still then that from outside I heard Rory's car. I heard it start, pull away, then speed up. I heard it pause at the gate, then go on. I wished I was with him, driving away from Rentlow Retreat forever.

I suddenly had a terrible feeling, a sick lost trembling intuition. Rory. Rory was gone. I would never see him again.

Jeremy said, "Teena love, it's all right. Nothing bad has happened, you know. In a little while, Rory will get used to the idea, and he'll still be our very good friend just as he's always been."

But I remembered Rory's look of pain, reproach. I wondered if Jeremy could be right.

"We must make plans," Aunt June said, her sunken blue eyes dull.

"Of course," Charles agreed.

"And notify Margaretha—as soon as we can, that is," Aunt June went on.

"Of course," Charles repeated.

"No need for Teena to await Margaretha's return. After all, six months . . ."

They went on speaking as if I had given my consent, or perhaps as if I weren't even there. I had the strange and familiar feeling that they were acting out pre-decided roles, and that only I didn't know the lines I must speak. It was all totally out of my hands. I knew they would hear nothing I told them. They had decided that I would marry Jeremy. I suddenly wondered why.

The next day, I didn't want to pose for Jeremy. I felt tired, strained, nervously aware of his possessive manner, and Estrella's uneasy tension, and Uncle Charles' very noticeable good cheer which underscored Aunt June's false enthusiam.

When I told Jeremy I'd prefer to skip the session, he frowned. "But Teena, it's important to stay on schedule. You don't realize, of course, but I can't work in fits and starts. I can't pick up and set down. We must go on today as always. I insist." His dark eyes glimmered with hot embers. His thin mouth twisted in an unconvincing smile.

"Couldn't it wait until tomorrow?" I asked hopelessly, knowing what his answer would be. And I was right.

"Why tomorrow?" he demanded. "How will it be different from today?"

"I might feel more like it," I told him.

"Oh, Jeremy," Estrella put in, surprising me, "why don't you leave her alone?"

And Aunt June said, "Yes, Jeremy dear, surely, if Teena doesn't feel like it . . ."

Jeremy divided a quick hard look between them. "I wish you two would mind your own business."

He put his arm around me and drew me with him. At the threshold, I turned to look back.

Estrella and June were watching, their faces pale and set, their bodies peculiarly rigid and unmoving.

I wore the white dress he insisted on. I sat in the pose he ordered. My head was tilted back, my hair flowing loose on my shoulders. I looked at the glowing white walls, and the shining black door past his shoulders.

He set to work, the mallet tapping.

He murmured to me; to himself.

I was drowsing, only partly aware of his voice.

The door suddenly opened. Mrs. Foxall peered in.

Jeremy glared at her, put down his mallet.

"Got to clean in here some time," she grumbled, her grapefruit-yellow face stolid.

"Not now," he said.

"They tell me you gave out some big news last night."

"That's right," he said.

"It's none of my business," she said, jerking her head at me, "but you're too young, Teena. You don't know what you're doing."

"That's right," he said before I could answer. "It's none of your business, Mrs. Foxall."

She stepped back, closing the door.

Jeremy sighed, took up the mallet and chisel again.

I still felt on my lips the light kiss he had pressed then when he had moved my shoulders, settled my arms as he wanted them.

His dark hair gleamed. His face was solemn, intent. His long slim hands moved smoothly, swiftly, as if operating with a will of their own.

Mrs. Foxall, limping from room to room, doing work she didn't have to do. Not when her husband owned a successful drugstore. Mrs. Foxall, watchful, ever-present, except after dark, skirting the hedge maze where her sister May Argon's statue stood, on the way to the tall iron gates and the safety of her husband's car beyond. Jimmie Hunnicut had told me why she worked in Rentlow Retreat. It was because of Sarah Calvert's death. First May's death ten years before, then Sarah Calvert's. Mrs. Foxall was suspicious of the Rentlows, and had warned me to go away, and seemed always to be looking, listening. I wondered what she was looking for; listening for. Something to do with Sarah? I found myself thinking then of Rory.

Rory, as I had first seen him, running into the airport waiting room, his auburn hair bright as a candle in the dark. Rory, breathless and smiling, and later on, driving up the coast, suddenly questioning and somber. Rory, within moments, someone I had known all my life, begging me to leave Rentlow Retreat. Was it because he had known that Jeremy would fall in love with me? Did he fear that because of his sister? Or did he fear that for some reason I couldn't imagine?

Suddenly I opened my eyes. I was dizzy. The room spun around me.

Jeremy was leaning over me, a hand on my shoulder. I felt its warmth through my dress. I felt the pressure of his fingers.

"All through," he said lightly, and brushed a kiss on my forehead. "You see how fast the time went?"

I blinked at him. "But we just started."

"Three hours ago."

I felt curiously depleted, and when I swallowed my throat hurt. There was a tiny sore place on my neck. I remembered feeling it before. I got to my feet, braced myself against the chair. Unsteady, cold, I said, "I think I'll go out for some fresh air."

"You mustn't go far," he told me. "You're tired, aren't you?"

I was always tired, I thought, as I went to my room. I changed into jeans and a shirt, tied my hair back in a ribbon. I tucked a book under my arm, and went outside.

Aunt June asked with false brightness, "All right, Teena?" and I nodded. After a moment, I said I would stretch my legs and left her. I went around the side of the house, past the garages and up to the ridge that overlooked the sea. I glanced up at Retreat Point, but sat down a good distance away from it, my book open on my lap. But I found that I couldn't read. My gaze went back, again and again, to the place where May Argon had jumped to her death, where Bethel Harper had accidentally fallen. Bethel Harper, an old family friend of the Rentlows, who had visited them for a week, and died, and been buried in Tumlee. Bethel Harper whose initials were the same as my father's. It *was* too much of a coincidence. What if they had been the same man? What if Ben had been here at Rentlow Retreat, and wired that he would meet me, and then, before he could, he died? I was tired, so terribly tense and tired. It was hard to think straight, to order my thoughts. The

98

third car still in the garage . . . Jeremy had said it belonged to Bethel. Something in it might prove that, or prove otherwise.

Rory had never seen Bethel, being away on a business trip for the week that Bethel was here, but he might know something, and I had promised him that I would tell him if I was worried, concerned, about anything, any time. He didn't realize how few opportunities there were for me to see him alone. I straightened up. I was alone now, and there was the shortcut. I decided to go to Rory's house.

I rose, edged past the rhododendron bushes that concealed the maze exit, scrambled along the ridge past Retreat Point and finally found the path that I knew must be the shortcut.

Stumbling, breathless, forcing my tired body to go on, I picked my way along until the faint path emerged from a grove of elms, and I saw the bright blue shutters, the white clapboard of Rory's home.

I hurried to the door, knocked, knocked again.

The silence disturbed me, but it was a silence different from that of Rentlow Retreat. Here at Rory's birds sang and the trees whispered. Here there was life. I pounded my fist against the door as hard as I could. The silence seemed to deepen as I waited, straining for a familiar footstep.

At last I forced myself to turn away.

Rory wasn't there.

But Jeremy stood at the porch steps, dark eyes regarding me intently. "I had an idea," he said, "that you might come here."

I was speechless with sudden fright, a fright I couldn't explain to myself.

"We'd better go home," he said, and took my limp hand.

But Rentlow Retreat wasn't home, I thought. It could never be. Not for me. It was dreary, and death-cursed. It filled me with unaccountable terror.

I gave Rory's flower-filled sunporch a last glance and found myself wondering if I would ever see it again.

"You're so quiet," Jeremy said, and he seemed to be

laughing. "I think your long walk must have quite taken your breath away."

Rory was on the terrace when we reached Rentlow Retreat. He wore tan trousers, a tan shirt. His dark auburn hair was brushed back from his rugged face. The contrast between him and Jeremy struck me forcibly as it had before. Rory seemed so strong, solid, thoughtful. Jeremy was the handsomer by far, and he was warm, persuasive. Yet, at odd moments, there was a glimmer in his eyes that chilled me.

It was there when he told Rory, "You'll be sorry to hear that you missed Teena. She went to visit you. And via the shortcut." He turned to me. "Teena, you must promise me you won't do that again. The ridge is dangerous for those that don't know it.'

I thought instantly of May Argon. She had surely known the ridge, yet she had died there. And then I thought of Bethel Harper . . .

Rory smiled at me. It was as if the evening before and the announcement of my engagement to Jeremy had never taken place. He said, "I'm sorry I wasn't there. I went to Tumlee, and stopped here on my way back."

Aunt June passed drinks and crackers, creating a diversion.

Then Rory asked, "I wondered if you'd set the date, Teena?"

"No." I took a deep breath, then said deliberately, "You see, I want my father to give me away, and my mother here too. Ben and Margaretha . . ."

Uncle Charles' gray eyes studied me coldly from behind his rimless glasses. "That's an extraordinary idea," he said at last.

Aunt June chimed in, "Teena, dear, you can't possibly be serious."

"I am," I said stubbornly. "They must be here with me, otherwise . . ."

"Apparently you don't understand," Uncle Charles said heavily. "There's a great enmity between your father and mother. That's why there's been no contact between them for all these years. Margaretha," Charles went on, "was money mad, you know. She drove and drove Ben, and finally, when he didn't produce, she left him for Arthur Haines. I never did approve. I don't now. But Ben swore he'd have no more to do with her, or with you, until he'd made his fortune."

"What happened to him?"

Uncle Charles shrugged. "He went off. He was never heard of again. So I suppose he was a failure later as he had been earlier."

"But he wired that he'd meet me," I protested.

Uncle Charles shrugged again. "I expect that was a whim and he regretted it. Which is why he never turned up."

I listened to Uncle Charles' words, and stored them away. Perhaps, I thought. But perhaps not. Perhaps Ben had showed up, and stayed here in Rentlow Retreat for a week, yes, stayed with his third cousin, Charles Rentlow, who'd first introduced him to Margaretha. And perhaps Ben had learned I was coming through the Rentlows, and wired that he'd meet me. And then, perhaps, he had died at Retreat Point, and been buried as Bethel Harper.

But why?

Why? Why should he have died just before I arrived? And why had I myself had two near misses with death just after I came? And why had I had no other near misses?

Questions that had no answers.

Speculations that had no proofs.

I shivered suddenly.

And Rory said, "I've been asked by Dr. Benson if I could bring you in to see him. Just a social call, Teena. He'd like to get to know you."

"I'd like that," I said, instantly aware of the opportunity a visit to Tumlee would give me.

"How about tomorrow?" Rory asked.

"Fine," I said quickly, hurrying to keep Jeremy from protesting that he, and only he, would take me to town.

But he simply smiled and sipped his drink.

Mrs. Foxall came out, closed the door hard behind her. She grunted a farewell, and went limping down the

101

driveway toward the gate. I noticed again, that as always, when she was abreast of the entrance to the maze, she increased her speed as much as she could, peering nervously at the tall hedges and the white fountain until she was well past them.

Jeremy caught me staring at her small back. He said softly, "A pity. She would be a fine subject for my gallery. Look at the shape of her. But she just won't agree."

Aunt June's glass fell from her fingers, shattered on the terrace.

Uncle Charles growled, "Really, dear, your nerves are unbelievably bad these days."

I knew before he went on what he would say.

"I think you should go with Rory and Teena tomorrow. You can consult with Dr. Benson. Perhaps he can give you something to calm you."

"Oh, no," she said, "I'm perfectly all right, Charles."

"I insist," he told her pleasantly. "Go in tomorrow with Rory and Teena."

There went my opportunity, I thought. I had so wanted to be alone with Rory for a little while, and even more, I had made plans. I would ask in Tumlee about Bethel Harper. I would find out if anyone had seen him, known him, spoke to him. Surely if he'd stayed at Rentlow Retreat for a week, he'd have left some trace in Tumlee. And if he had, then perhaps I could identify him more clearly. I could find out what he looked like, where he had come from. I could find out if he could possibly have been my father, been using another name for some reason of his own.

But, the next day, when Rory came for me, Aunt June was ready and waiting for him.

As we drove into Tumlee I thought of the last time he had brought me in, and wished more than ever that we had somehow managed to be alone.

Rory said he had errands and dropped us off at Dr. Benson's house.

Aunt June seemed glad to see him. When she smiled I suddenly saw a faint echo of Margaretha's beauty in her face. I wondered what had aged her so. Margaretha hadn't seen June in so many years, she couldn't have known how she was now, I thought.

Dr. Benson plucked his lips, and chuckled, when Aunt June explained that we were a team, one half on a professional call and one half on a social visit. He suggested that the professional part be disposed of first, since as a widower he was inclined to like to savor company at his leisure. The faint pleasure was gone from Aunt June's face when she allowed herself to be led unwillingly down the hall to the office, first asking, "You'll wait right here, won't you, Teena?"

Although I nodded a positive agreement, I waited only until the frosted door was closed behind her. Then I slipped out. The street was empty. Rory's car wasn't in sight as I hurried to the post office.

CHAPTER ELEVEN

The man behind the high wooden counter nodded briefly at me. He had a round bald head and pale eyes under gray brows. I saw by the metal plate that stood over a pile of stamps that his name was Mr. Jessup.

I said, "Mr. Jessup, I'm Teena Halliday. I wonder if you'd answer a question for me."

"Eh?" he shouted. "What's the matter? What did you say?"

I raised my voice. "I'm Teena Halliday. Can you tell me please if you ever had any mail for Bethel Harper?"

His gray brows went up quizzically. "Seems to me that's no business of yours. Since you're not Bethel Harper, as I happen to know."

"Did you ever see him?" I asked quickly.

"Didn't," Mr. Jessup answered.

"He was never in here?"

"Never."

I was ready to go, sagging with disappointment. Then another question occurred to me. I asked, "What about Ben Halliday, Mr. Jessup? Did you ever get any mail for him? Or see him?"

"Ben Halliday? Ben? Is that what you said?"

I nodded.

"Not for a Ben Halliday," he told me.

It was obviously no use. I left the post office, telling myself that there were still plenty of places to try. I went to the general store. The woman at the cash register stared at me suspiciously.

I introduced myself, knowing it wasn't necessary. Plainly everybody in Tumlee knew who I was. I said, "I've been wondering, did Bethel Harper, the man that visited Rentlow Retreat, ever come here?"

"Not that you'd notice. If he spent any money in this town it was elsewhere, and I never heard of it. And I just told as much to Rory Calvert. If you don't believe me, then ask him."

Rory. So Rory had had the same idea that I had. Or was that it? Was that why he was asking about Bethel Harper?

I hurried outside. But he still wasn't in sight.

I turned into Foxall's Drugstore. Mr. Foxall nodded at me, said, "You're peaked, Teena Halliday. Just as the wife told me."

I asked him about Bethel Harper.

Mr. Foxall shook his head. "All I know is what the wife told me."

The door opened suddenly. Jimmie Hunnicut slipped in, stood there, peering at me from bright blue eyes.

I tried to smile at him, but my lips felt stiff. My whole body felt worn down by disappointment. It seemed as if I would never find anyone who could tell me about Bethel Harper.

Jimmie said, "Mr. Jessup at the post office just told Mrs. Bagley from the library that you were asking about that man Bethel Harper."

I nodded.

"Then you'd better go see my dad, hadn't you?"

"Your dad?"

"At Hunnicut's Service Station," Jimmie told me. "It's down the highway. I'll take you straight to it, if you want."

"You'd better stay out of grownups' business," Mr.

Foxall put in. "Especially when that business concerns Rentlow Retreat."

But I was impressed by Jimmie's idea. Bethel Harper had had a car. It was still in the Rentlows' garage.

Jimmie and I hurried to his father's station. Mr. Hunnicut listened, scratched his head, said, "No, I can't think what my boy has in mind. I never had Bethel Harper as a customer. I'd have remembered, you see. I'd have recalled it surely when he died." He paused, thought for a moment. "Yes, I'm certain. We have so few strangers hereabouts. There was only one along then. A big man, gray-haired. Laughed a lot. And rich by the look of it. Paid with a credit card."

A big man who laughed a lot . . . Mrs. Foxall had told me almost the same thing about Bethel Harper.

"Did you get his name?" I asked quickly.

"Honey," Mr. Hunnicut drawled, "I wouldn't recall. How could I? It was weeks and weeks ago."

"But you're sure that it wasn't Bethel Harper?"

"Indeed I'm sure of that."

"Could it have been Ben Halliday?"

Mr. Hunnicut shot me a quick look. "It could have been just about anybody, honey."

Jimmie piped up, "You could look, Dad. You've got the carbons of the credit card sales."

"I could," Mr. Hunnicut agreed. "But I'm busy now on a big job, and besides that, I don't like to get mixed up in Rentlow Retreat stuff. The less I have to do with those folks the better I like it." He turned his eyes down to Jimmie. "And that goes for you too."

"It couldn't do any harm to know who that stranger was," Jimmie insisted.

I held my breath until Mr. Hunnicut sighed, said, "okay, I'll just have a look."

I held my breath again while he flipped through a big box of receipts, mumbling to himself, "No, no, and no . . . ." Finally he said, "Oh, yes, here it is." He looked up at me, frowning. "What was the name you asked me? Ben Halliday? Well, that's right. That's who he was. Is he a relative of yours?"

His words swept over me, a drowning wave of sudden truth, suspicions confirmed too terrible to be borne.

Bethel Harper and Ben Halliday were the same man.

And Bethel Harper was dead. Which meant that Ben Halliday was dead.

I thanked Mr. Hunnicut, thanked Jimmie, and made my way slowly back to Dr. Benson's house.

Ben had come to Rentlow Retreat. He must have learned from the Rentlows that I was expected. He must have wired me that he'd meet me, and then . . .

But how was I to prove it? What was I to do?

From a block away, I saw Rory, saw how he was staring down the street, how he rushed to meet me, his long legs carrying him forward in quick strides.

"Teena, Aunt June's about to have a fit," he said.

"Sorry, I had something to do . . . I couldn't . . ."

"I know. I know. You were asking about Bethel. There isn't time now to explain. Don't tell the Rentlows, Teena. Don't say a word, and for God's sake, don't sit for Jeremy any more."

I had no chance to answer. Rory rushed me back to Dr. Benson's house. Aunt June and the doctor were on the porch.

"You see?" Rory said. "She just decided to take a small walk."

"Teena Halliday," Aunt June gasped, "whatever could you have been thinking of? Why, we came out of the doctor's office, and you were gone. Gone." She seemed almost in tears, her lips trembling, her face gray.

I apologized and explained that I'd thought of something I wanted to buy at Mr. Foxall's.

"And did you get it?" she demanded, with a glance at my empty hands.

"He didn't have it," I explained, annoyed with myself for not having thought to pick up something that would have served to make my explanation more believable. As it was, Aunt June clearly didn't take my words at face value.

She said, "I think we'd better go home now."

"Nonsense," Dr. Benson said. He made a flapping motion with his arms that moved us inside. "We have

106

to have tea and cookies. And if you don't allow this old widower to exhibit his culinary skills he'll be more than put out with you."

He settled us in his living room, which, unlike that of most widowers, had a comfortable and lived-in air. Within moments he had proudly brought in a tea tray and had us all served.

I nibbled a cookie and sipped tea, hardly noticing what I was doing. My thoughts whirled with questions. Could I be sure beyond doubt that Bethel Harper and my father were the same man? Why would the Rentlows have pretended that they hadn't heard from my father for twelve years? What had happened to him? Why had Rory ordered me to say nothing? Why had he begged me not to sit any more for Jeremy?

I glanced sideways at Rory, wishing I could ask him. But Aunt June had taken a seat close to me, and watched me with haggard eyes, as if determined that I not escape her for a second time.

But I did. We had finished tea and were chatting when Dr. Benson said, "While you're here, Teena, I'll have a look at your shoulder."

"It's fine," I protested. "I've forgotten all about it."

"But I haven't seen it since I took out the stitches. And I think a checkup is due." He paused, then said, "Besides, you look rather pale to me, possibly too thin."

"These young girls," Aunt June sighed. "You know what they are, Doctor. They just don't eat properly." She rose. "And I do think we must go."

But he had assumed his physician's impervious manner, and with a quick gesture, he waved me into the hall, and down it to his office.

There, with the frosted door closed behind him, he said, "We don't have a great deal of time. June is restless. So don't interrupt me with questions. Just get on the scale, please."

My mouth opened to protest, I found myself being weighed. Then I was sitting in a chair. He put a firm hand under my chin, tipped my head back. He raised my eyelids, peered down at me. He moved my lips back and examined my gums.

He said, "Let me tell you, Rory was in yesterday. He said he was worried about you. At how you look to him. I told him we'd see. I want to do a blood test."

"But . . ."

"Teena, please." He moved away, spoke over his shoulder, while his hands moved quickly over a big white tray. "Your weight is down, of course. Surely you hit about a hundred and five. The scales show a bit less than a hundred now. Your gums aren't as red as they should be, nor the membranes in your eyes. You feel tired all the time, don't you, Teena?" He came toward me, a needle in his hand. "Now then, make a fist, and bend your arm."

I automatically obeyed him. The needle stung slightly. The tube filled slowly with my blood. I had to look away from it.

"Besides being tired, Teena, what else do you feel?"

"I . . . just that," I said. "And breathless sometimes. And . . ."

He withdrew the needle, set it aside, patted my arm with a bit of alcohol-saturated cotton. "This is just to make sure. But I am quite sure already. You're run-down, anemic. As if you've lost a lot of blood." He drew a long slow breath. "We'll have to see about this. Meanwhile I'm going to give you iron pills. I want you to take them regularly. And I want you to get a lot of rest. A lot of it, Teena. I don't want you to do much of anything." His white head was bent close to me. His voice was a whisper. "Do you understand? Not much of anything. I especially don't want you to strain yourself by sitting for the figure Jeremy is doing for you. Rory told me about it, and I feel you shouldn't strain yourself that way right now. Though you needn't say that. I suggest you simply make your excuses and avoid it."

"Rory told you . . . He asked you to look at me . . ."

I was puzzled, but immeasurably happy. Rory hadn't turned his back on me when Jeremy announced our engagement. Rory *was* my ally. He was worried about me. Later it occurred to me to wonder why his concern made me happy. And it occurred to wonder why he and Dr. Benson insisted that I must not let Jeremy work on the figure of me any more. But then, at that moment, there were too many other things on my mind.

"Do you think something is wrong with me?" I asked fearfully. The thought of being ill and at the mercy of Rentlow Retreat was almost paralyzing.

"I don't know." He leaned close to me, tipped my head back again, peered at my throat. "What's this pin-prick here? How long have you had it?"

"I don't know, Doctor. I don't remember. It's just always been there, I guess."

"We'd better go back. And you needn't mention this to your Aunt June. It would only worry her, and her nerves are already bad."

He waved me ahead of him. But it was my turn to hesitate. From nowhere, unbidden, without any explanation that I could see, a sudden thought had come to me. I put it into words. "Dr. Benson, did you treat Sarah Calvert when she was ill?"

He gave me a long, deep, and penetrating look. Then he nodded, and before I could ask any more, he had turned away, chuckling loudly. "You heal beautifully, Teena," he was saying, as he entered the living room. "I'm pleased with my hemstitching, I must confess."

Jeremy had been insistent that I pose for him that afternoon, but I had refused to. I had refused to firmly, excusing myself on the grounds of being tired out by my visit to Tumlee with Aunt June and Rory. He had finally shrugged and said, "Teena love, if that's how a small journey to town takes you, then I'm afraid we must see that you don't go any more." I understood that as the threat it was meant to be. My heart sank. How was I to find out about my father? He had been at Hunnicut's in Tumlee. Then surely he had come to Rentlow Retreat. And surely there had not been any two visitors here. Not two with the same initials. Which meant that Bethel Harper and Ben Halliday must be the same man. Then what had happened? Why? There must be something in Rentlow Retreat, I thought suddenly, that would show my father had been here. If I

109

couldn't go to Tumlee, then I must search Rentlow Retreat, But how could I? I told myself that I must.

Jeremy was asking insistently, "You do see why you can't go to Tumlee any more, don't you?"

"Oh, it wasn't that," I protested. "I'm just not in the mood. Sitting so still isn't pleasant for me, Jeremy."

"Poor darling," he grinned. "I'm so sorry. Perhaps a day off will do you some good. Just remember, though, you do it for me, to make me happy. And you do want to make me happy, don't you?"

I pretended not to hear the mockery in his voice. I smiled at him, and then I went up to my room to lie down on the bed.

Chill wrapped me in an invisible blanket as I tried to sort my thoughts. The first night I had come, I had thought I'd heard a voice call to me, my name whispered in the stormy dark below. I'd opened the casement, and the whole window had dropped away from my weight. If I hadn't clung to the velvet drapes, I would have fallen to the terrace below. And so soon after, I moved my library books on the mantel and the huge gold-framed mirror tipped and fell free. If Rory hadn't been with me, if he hadn't lunged across the room, swept me up into his arms and away, I'd have been crushed under the shattering glass, not just cut by a flying shard. After that? Nothing. Nothing. Jeremy had gone to work sculpting me. Nothing more had happened. But I had lost weight, grown unaccountably tired. Jeremy had announced our engagement, an engagement that I hadn't actually considered or agreed to. And no one seemed to notice my reluctance.

Now Rory and Dr. Benson had warned me not to sit for Jeremy any more. Just as Rory and Mrs. Foxall had warned me to leave Rentlow Retreat.

The thought of Rory warmed me against the chill that enwrapped me. I examined the feeling with wonder. I found that I hungered to see him, to speak to him, to touch him. I hungered to feel the safety of his arms around me again. I hoped that now, at home in his office or working in the flower-filled sunporch, he was thinking of me.

But then I thought of Estrella, her possessive hand on his arm, her possessive dark eyes, and her voice sweet and low saying to Rory that she understood how he must think of Sarah when Jeremy announced his engagement to me, think of Sarah and her slow death. Obviously that's just what Rory was thinking of, I told myself, suddenly chilled again. He was obsessed with what had happened to her. He had even talked about me with Dr. Benson because Dr. Benson had treated her.

I sat up, swung my feet to the green carpet.

I wasn't Sarah Calvert. I wasn't even the same Teena Halliday who had fearfully boarded the airplane in Rome, weeping to say goodbye to Maria and Tony. I was on my own, I knew, and couldn't tug at Margaretha's apron strings to ask what I should do.

I had to stop thinking about Sarah. Whatever had happened to her had nothing to do with me. I mustn't think of her, of her tilted-back head and unseeing eyes that stared forever at the ceiling of Jeremy's gallery, and I mustn't think of slender May Argon standing frozen beneath the sky in the tall hedge maze, and I mustn't think of poor little Scuffy posed on the smooth green lawn that was Jeremy's animal cemetery. I mustn't ask myself why Estrella had wanted to know if I had other family, friends, to whom I could go, and why she feared Jeremy.

I had to concentrate on only one thing. I must see if my father had left any trace of his presence in Rentlow Retreat.

I went to my bedroom door. The house was still. I stepped outside, peering along the shadowed hall.

Jeremy's studio door was firmly closed.

I tiptoed past it, then past the alcove where the desk barred the stairs to the attic. It was one place Estrella hadn't taken me on the tour of the house, and I remembered now how she had seemed to hurry me away from it. I determined to have a look at it now.

I reached past the desk, turned the knob on the attic door. It swung open. I dropped down, crept under the desk and into what seemed like a small closet. I got up, eased the door shut, and found a light switch beside it. When the dull bulb glowed I saw the steps leading upward.

I followed them to a big, nearly empty room. There, set aside against a wall under the window, was a quilt-covered stack. I went to it first and threw back the quilt.

It had covered two suitcases. I bent over them, and caught my breath.

Each was initialed in worn gold. B. H.

B. H. for Bethel Harper? Or for Ben Halliday?

There were no shipping tags on the handles, no identifying marks at all. I opened both cases quickly and peered in at the neatly packed clothes within. Slowly, with my hands suddenly cold, I searched through the clothes, personal belongings, that might have belonged to a stranger. Or might have belonged to my father. Nothing, nothing gave me a clue, until once again, on silver-backed hair brushes, I saw the initials. B. H. I re-packed the suitcases slowly, thinking that it was impossible that the duplication of the initials was a simple coincidence. And if I was right, then my father was dead, and buried under the name of Bethel Harper.

Then why, why all the lies? I asked myself.

I replaced the quilt over the suitcases and crept down the stairs. I turned out the light, eased the door open, and crawled under the desk. I closed the door in the alcove, and hurried down to Uncle Charles' study. It was the only place else I could think of in which I might find some clue to what had happened, and why.

I listened outside the door for a moment, but I heard no sound. I slipped quickly inside, my heart pounding. The room was empty. I hurried to the desk. Its drawers were locked. I considered forcing them with a letter opener, but realized that would give me away to Uncle Charles. As I stood there, hesitating, I saw a piece of paper on the floor, a bit of bright color. I picked it up, stared at it.

I recognized it instantly as a piece of canceled stamp, a foreign stamp. When I examined it closely I could make out a few letters: "ilia." For Brasilia . . .

Margaretha and Timothy had left for South America the day I left for the United States. Margaretha had promised to write me as soon as she had an address. I had wondered why it had taken so long for me to hear from her. And in Tumlee's post office, I suddenly remembered, Mr. Jessup had demanded, "Ben Halliday? *Ben* Halliday, you say?" when I asked if there had been any mail for my father. I hadn't noticed the stress on that first name, but I recalled it now and understood. He had seen a letter, or letters, for me, for *Teena* Halliday. The bit of postage stamp in my fingers proved it.

Margaretha had written to me. I simply hadn't received her letters. They'd been picked up at the post office with the other Rentlow mail, and destroyed.

I heard a sound in the hallway.

As I hurried from Uncle Charles' study, Mrs. Foxall said, "I hear you've been to town."

I nodded, brushed by her, and went upstairs, anxious to reach the sanctuary of my room.

But once there, I found Jeremy. He turned from the window, regarding me with sparkling eyes. "You seem to have quite recovered," he said.

CHAPTER TWELVE

May Argon, and Sarah Calvert, and Scuffy walked stiffly along the ridge. From Retreat Point, a tall blond man watched them. A plump woman with a tower of purple hair whispered a single word, a word I couldn't quite hear . . .

I awakened suddenly, relieved to be free of an unpleasant dream.

The sun was bright on the carpet, chips of gold in the motes that danced above it.

I sat up, swung my feet to the floor, humming a song that Maria used to sing to me when I was a small child. In a minute, I thought, I'd call Maria and she'd bring me rolls and a tiny cup of coffee, and then . . .

And then reality touched me. I was not at home in the villa. The hot sunlight on the carpet was not the Mediterranean sun. I couldn't call Maria, for she wouldn't hear me.

The nightmare from which I'd awakened was more real than these moments of homesick illusion.

The sun was no longer as bright. I found myself shivering.

I had slept heavily, but I was still tired. I took the thick red iron pills that Dr. Benson had given me the day before. I wondered if they would help me. I wondered if he had given them to Sarah too, and waited to see what would happen while she slowly faded away.

Once again, as in my dream, I saw May Argon, and Sarah, and Scuffy walking stiffly along the ridge. They were shadowed white, chiseled marble, the stone in which Jeremy had carved them.

I gripped the edge of the dressing table and clenched my chattering teeth. I heard Mrs. Bagley say, "You might be interested in those." I saw her purple towered head incline toward shelves nearby, and squinted at them. VAMPIRES, WEREWOLVES, AND SUCCUBI.

Huge, horror-filled eyes peered at me from my reflection. My gaunt face was gray.

A wave of sickness engulfed me. I knew that I must be losing my mind. Something terrible, unexplainable, had happened to me in Rentlow Retreat. How else could I explain to myself what I was thinking?

I fought the sickness and conquered it. I resolutely argued my terror away. May Argon had been eccentric, perhaps retarded, and committed suicide. Sarah Calvert had died of a blood disorder. Scuffy had been ill. These were things that had simply happened. They had nothing to do with Jeremy's gallery, nor the green sloping lawn, nor the tall hedge maze. Mrs. Foxall, all the others in the town, had been infected by a kind of hysteria because the Rentlows kept to themselves. Yes, yes, I persuaded myself, I had no reason to fear Jeremy.

I must concentrate on the real, not on mad imaginings. I must find out what happened to my father after he stopped at Hunnicut's station. I must discover why the Rentlows had never given me Margaretha's letters. I knew what I had to do, but I didn't know where to begin.

I dressed slowly, putting on blue jeans, a white shirt, sneakers. I bound my hair back in a white ribbon. I powdered my pale face and etched a bright mouth on my too-faded lips.

114

Briefly, as I opened the door to the hallway, the song Maria sang to me when I was a small child echoed in my head, and tears stung my eyes. It was part of the past to which I would never return.

Jeremy came out of his studio as I started down the hall. There was a faint film of powder on his hands, white and fine. It dusted his dark trousers and his shirt. Even his lips seemed to glimmer with it. He had been working. That was obvious. I tried not to shudder.

He said, "Up early today, aren't you, Teena love? Your rest must have done you a lot of good."

"Oh, yes, thanks," I told him.

"Then we must make up for lost time."

"No, Jeremy, I don't want to pose for you today. It's lovely out of doors. I want to go and wander in the sun alone for a while."

"But, Teena love, you must. I've explained to you . . ."

There was nothing to be afraid of, I told myself firmly. Jeremy couldn't hurt me. I had allowed myself to become prey to sick imaginings, to a madness that I must control.

But Rory had warned me not to sit for Jeremy any more, and asked Dr. Benson to check me over. Dr. Benson had treated Sarah Calvert for a strange blood problem, and now he said that I was anemic, and suggested that I not mention it to the others. There was some explanation. Not the sick thoughts in my mind, the dream-festering thoughts. There was some sensible reason for Rory's warning.

I smiled as apologetically as I could at Jeremy. "I'm sorry. Some other time."

"I don't understand," he said.

I shrugged and started down the steps.

He followed me closer than I would have liked, so close that I could feel his touch, though in fact he did not touch me. It was like an emanation coming from him, brushing the back of my neck. "Teena, please, what's the matter?"

"Nothing. I just want . . ." I laughed a little. "I don't know, Jeremy. I don't want to stay inside today. We'll have plenty of time."

"Oh, yes. We will. Forever." But he put a hand on my shoulder. "Why, Teena. What's wrong?"

115

"Nothing, Jeremy."

He peered into my eyes. "Ever since you went into town with Rory yesterday . . ."

"I don't know what you mean."

"Since then . . ." Jeremy repeated softly, fingers, suddenly tight and bruising. Then, "Teena love, is it Rory? Is it something he said to you?"

I found myself backed against the wall, hemmed in, imprisoned. I tried to look away from Jeremy's hot burning eyes, but the very insistence that I feared compelled me.

He murmured, "Poor child, you don't really understand, do you? I haven't wanted to say anything. None of us has wanted to. After all, Rory has been our friend for so long, so very long, and then he and Estrella . . . but you see, Teena, he's become very morbid lately. Very morbid indeed. I'm afraid, yes, I might as well be honest with you; I must be honest with you. I'm quite afraid that in his heart, in some deep and hidden place, he's come to hate me. Because of Sarah, you see. He always felt . . . forgive me, Teena, perhaps you can't see this, that Sarah belonged to him. And then she fell in love with me. We became engaged. Poor Rory. He was distraught. And she became ill. She just . . ." Jeremy shook his dark head. He closed his eyes momentarily, his thin mouth drawn tight with pain.

"It was unbearable. And still is. But we've had to bear it. To accept it. Sarah died. Rory couldn't accept it. I'm sure, I'm certain, though he pretends differently, that he blames me out of his old jealousy. And now that he sees that you love me, and I love you, something terrible and twisted has grown up in his mind. He hates the thought that we'll marry and be happy. He hates it so much that he'd do anything to prevent it. You won't let him, will you, Teena? You won't let him destroy us?"

My lips were numb. My throat was tight. My breath fought my taut throat in aching pressure. I shook my head blindly, whispered, "No, Jeremy, I won't. I won't."

I meant my answer only to silence him, to give me a chance to escape. But there was acquiescence in it too. Ugly doubt whispered, "Rory warned you against the

116

Rentlows, warned you not to commit yourself to anything, thinking of Jeremy . . . and that was when he first met you. Why, Teena? How could he have guessed what would happen? Why, Teena?"

"You'd think a body would find a better place to talk than on the stairs," Mrs. Foxall said suddenly, looking up at us.

I didn't know when she had come there or what she might have heard. I was only grateful for the interruption.

I stumbled down the steps, seeing her quick sideways look at me, realizing then what I had noticed so many times before. Mrs. Foxall seemed to be a dozen places at once. She was here, there, and everywhere, always watching, always listening. Jimmie Hunnicut had told me why. Was she, as I had insisted to myself earlier, infected by some weird and unreasoning fear of the Rentlows, or did she have a rational basis for her suspicions?

Jeremy padded along behind me. I hurried to the door. He was with me when I opened it. I said, "Jeremy, please, I just want to be alone for a little while."

"Of course," he said gently, his dark eyes sparkling. "I think I understand. Go ahead, Teena love. You know that whatever you want, I want. Whatever you need, that's all I'll ever need."

I ducked my head at him and forced myself to walk slowly across the terrace, feeling his gaze on my back until I turned the corner of the house.

The garage caught my eyes. The third car was still parked there. Bethel Harper's car. Or had it been Ben Halliday's? It crossed my mind that I ought to search it, but I could think of nothing, no one, except Rory, and what Jeremy had just told me.

Rory had warned me away from Rentlow Retreat at the moment of my arrival. He had begged me to trust him as a friend, but he hadn't told me about his sister's death, nor her engagement to Jeremy. Rory had pretended to care for me; yes, yes, I could see that he had, but at the same time he had always courted Estrella. He listened to my suspicions, asked questions in Tumlee, even spoke to Dr. Benson. But he had never told me what I must fear, what danger lay in wait for me. Plainly, and it seemed terribly true in that moment, he wanted only to make sure that I didn't marry Jeremy. Not for my safety, not for love of me. But because he hated Jeremy.

It fit so perfectly. I wondered why I hadn't realized before what drove Rory. I supposed that I hadn't wanted to. I finally allowed myself for the first time to face the fact that all the time I had been drawn to Jeremy, had allowed him to announce our engagement, I had somehow had a hope in my heart that involved Rory. I gave that hope up now. And I gave up, too, the conviction that Rory was my ally, would help me.

Desolate, and frightened, and not knowing what to do, I stumbled through the trees and brush, finding my way to the ridge.

The cliff looked black, shadowed, dropping away below my feet. I peered up at Retreat Point. There, I thought, May Argon had stood before she died. Thinking what? And there, too, Bethel Harper—or had it been my father? —who stood there?

A shudder touched me. I saw on an empty screen before my burning eyes a slim body spilling awkwardly through the pale air. I saw blonde hair flowing and slender limbs beating uncaring emptiness. I saw a black stain on the jagged rocks that reached up, to pierce, to destroy it . . .

But the black spot moved. An arm lifted. A small tow-head tilted upward from the long elbow-like arm that separated the cove below into Rentlow Retreat and Calvert land.

Jimmie Hunnicut waggled his hand, gesturing at me.

I waved at him. Then I threw a quick glance back at the house. I thought I saw a face peer out at me from a lower floor window. I dropped to all fours so that I wouldn't be visible, hoping that it would seem I had simply sat down on the rocks. Still on all fours I crept along the ridge and down the path to the shore below.

Jimmie awaited me nervously. The freckles stood out on his face. His blue eyes searched the path behind me.

"It's Rory Calvert," Jimmie said finally, having made certain that I was alone. "He asked me to tell you he's finding out. He said you shouldn't do anything. That's what he said. Not anything, Teena."

"But . . ."

"My father called him," Jimmie explained. "About that name on the charge. Because if that man was Bethel Harper, then . . ." His thin, small-boy voice faded. "They thought it was important. So Rory asked me to come. He'll be there, he told me to tell you. He'll be there, but you just don't do anything. Right?"

I hesitated for a long moment. After what Jeremy had told me, dare I trust Rory? I didn't know. I couldn't know. But only he could find out about my father for me. Only Rory . . .

I said, "Can you go back to him now? Can you give him a message for me?"

Jimmie nodded. "I will."

"Tell him to ask at the post office if there was ever any mail for me. For *me,* Jimmie. And tell him, maybe, through the charge, he could . . . he could find out where my father is."

"My Dad already told him that. They're working on it." Jimmie swallowed. "And my Dad said you be careful. He told me to specially tell you."

Sudden tears stung my eyes. I wasn't as alone as I'd thought.

Jimmie gasped, said, "I'd better get going," and scrambled over the rocks toward the Calvert house.

"Hardly eats more than a bird," Mrs. Foxall grumbled at me. "I don't see why I cook it to throw it away, and leave dirty pots and pans behind. Why don't I just take it from the refrigerator and dump it in the garbage and have done with it?"

"I'm sorry," I said. "I guess I'm just not very hungry."

"Never very hungry," she retorted. "No wonder you're shrinking down to where I can hardly see you without my glasses. What would you expect? What would you think?"

Jeremy cut in, smiling thinly. "All right, Mrs. Foxall, we get your point. Teena will do better tomorrow, I'm sure." His dark eyes turned to me. "You will, won't you, Teena love?"

119

Estrella cut in impatiently, "Teena, when you saw Rory yesterday, did he say he'd be over? He didn't come by last night, and I thought surely he would. And I called him but the line's been busy for hours."

"He didn't say," I told Estrella. "But maybe your mother . . ."

"Mother's down with a headache." Estrella grimaced. "A lot of good it did for her to visit Dr. Benson. She ended up coming home sick."

Jeremy shrugged. "You know how she is. Things upset her." He turned to me, smiled. "You know what I've been thinking, Teena? I mean since you left me on the steps this morning and took yourself to the ridge? I just realized what the trouble is. I don't know why I've been so dense about it before."

"The trouble?" I asked blankly.

"Why you're so overwrought," he said. "You are, you know. Edgy, nervous." His smile widened. "It's typical for a young bride. The suspense, of course. The waiting. Nothing else. We ought to set the date, Teena, and then you can begin to plan your wedding, and everything will be all right."

"Oh, yes," Estrella cried. "That's a marvelous idea, Jeremy." She leaned towards me. "We'll have a wonderful time, Teena. We'll go shopping in Boston." Her face glowed with the thought of getting away from Rentlow Retreat for a while. She went on joyfully, "We can do all kinds of things, see some movies, and have lunches, and visit the museums, and I'll help you pick out whatever you need, and . . ."

Jeremy said meaningfully, "You might begin to do some shopping for yourself, Estrella."

She said, the glow gone, "Jeremy, you know that Rory . . ."

"A man sometimes has to be brought to the point. Suppose I speak to him."

By then, I had found my breath. I had fought down waves of revulsion and terror. I said as quietly as I could, "Jeremy, just a minute. I told you I want Margaretha here with me, and I want my father to give me away. I told you that I wasn't willing to set a date yet."

120

"But why not, Teena love?"

"I've just explained."

"You can't seriously expect that I'll wait the six months until your mother finishes her own honeymoon," he said silkily. "Or until, if ever, your father should turn up."

It was on the tip of my tongue to tell him that he would wait for me forever, because I would never marry him. It was on the tip of my tongue then to tell him to forget we'd ever been engaged. But I remembered Rory's warning. I swallowed hard and finally said only, "I want to wait for them, Jeremy."

Estrella's brittle laugh broke the silence. "I guess I have a little more time," she said.

The terrace was empty, peaceful. The green lawn was a still smooth blanket on which the white statues gleamed, forever motionless in hot sunlight. The tall black gates were shut, sealing the only breach in the high wall that surrounded the estate in a half circle that ran all the way to the ridge over the sea. Rentlow Retreat was well named, I thought, as I looked out of my window. But it could better be named Rentlow Prison.

I sighed, wondering if Rory had any news yet. I couldn't quite imagine what he was doing. Except that, if Jimmie had told me rightly, Rory was trying to help me. *If* Jimmie had told me rightly . . . And if Rory were really to be trusted. I crushed the tiny doubt into nothingness and instantly felt better. As soon as he could, he would come. He must be doing something important. Estrella had complained again that she couldn't reach him on the phone. Yes, he would come when he could. The assurances that I gave myself were small prayers offered to heaven, tokens of the faith to which I found myself clinging more and more.

Jeremy's low, intense voice broke into my musing. "Teena love, surely you're not going to hide in here all day. Come on. I want you to pose for me now. And no excuses, mind you. No excuses at all."

"Later," I said tiredly.

"I insist, Teena."

Rory's warning echoed in my mind.

121

"Please . . . I just can't."

Jeremy thrust the door open, stood there, staring at me, his dark eyes glittering, his mouth thinned and hard. "Teena, what *is* it?"

I felt a film of perspiration on my upper lip. I felt a wave of heat spill over me, then fade beneath a chilling wave of cold. I said, "Jeremy, I understand how you feel, how much you want to work. But I just don't want to pose today."

"That's what you said yesterday too. Yesterday, and now again today." His eyes narrowed. "Why? Why not? What do you think you're waiting for? Why is a delay desirable to you?"

"Delay?" I asked quickly. "I don't know what you mean."

"Of course you do." His voice dropped, crooned, "Teena love, you can tell me. What's in your mind, dear? After all, if you can't speak to me, tell me . . ."

I shook my head, at a loss for words, for further excuses.

"Put on the white dress," he told me. "Brush your hair. I'll be waiting for you."

He stepped outside and closed the door behind him. I could hear the movement of his shoulders as he leaned against it.

Plainly I had no choice. Or if I did, I didn't know what it was. He was watching me too carefully, already suspicious that I had changed, that something had happened, that I was waiting for a freedom he could only guess at.

I remembered Rory's warning, but I knew that I had to allay Jeremy's growing suspicion. There was only one way. I changed as he'd told me to, and then went out to him.

Unwillingly, but docile now, I followed him down the hall and into his studio.

He settled me in the chair, went to the big table. He took up the mallet, long hands caressing it. "Comfortable, Teena? Are you sure? I do want you to be completely comfortable, you know."

I murmured that I was, certain that if I nodded, shifted

122

my position in any way, he would turn a cold hard withering look on me.

"Lovely, Teena. How beautiful you are. I knew the very first moment I saw you . . ." His low, murmuring voice went on and on. The mallet tapped on and on. I found it hard to listen, to understand. I seemed to be drifting, dizzily spinning within the glow of the white walls. From a great distance, a single word caught my attention, a name held me. I strained to concentrate.

". . . Sarah," Jeremy was saying. "That's why Rory's so odd now, just as I told you. Estrella refuses to understand it. So she's a bit jealous of you, or at least she was until she realized that it wasn't actually you that Rory was interested in. It's only Sarah, of course. And always has been. But Sarah's dead now. She was beautiful too, you know, Teena. But she *is* dead." The mallet tapped on and on. Jeremy's voice went on and on. "Oh, yes, Sarah's dead, and you mustn't think that you can depend on Rory. There's nobody but us, Teena, nobody but you and me."

CHAPTER THIRTEEN

Jeremy's voice went on.

I clung to a single thought. Sarah was dead, and May Argon was dead, and Scuffy was dead too.

I saw the shiny black door behind Jeremy's shoulder. The door that led to his gallery. Within it there was the statue of Sarah, her head tilted back, her hair flowing on her shoulders.

The glow of the white walls grew stronger, more blinding. The tap of the mallet continued, along with the hypnotic croon of Jeremy's voice. I felt like a distant observer, watching my awareness as a tiny candle flame that flickered and danced. I tried to concentrate on it with all my strength, soundlessly whispering, Sarah, Sarah, what happened to you? Was it here? In this room? What happened to you? To the others? Sarah . . . Sarah . . .

I was unable to move, to speak.

Jeremy's low murmuring voice, the sound of the mallet, the shadows reaching . . .

Then his lips were at my throat.

And some time later I suddenly saw the pale lemon sunlight that streaked the bare dark floor.

I heard a humming silence.

I was weary, weak, uncertain. But I clung to faint recollections of his kiss, and my fingers trembled at the place he had touched.

I fought the terrible tiredness that I recognized now. The drained weakness that I understood and accepted as proof of the unbelievable truth.

It was a truth that seemed like madness. So much like madness that I dared not scream my accusation aloud.

Who would listen?

Who would believe me?

But I couldn't doubt my certainty.

I knew now what the animal graveyard stood for.

I knew now what caused the dread in Aunt June's eyes, and Estrella's poised nervousness.

I knew what must have happened to May Argon so long before, and why she had talked so wildly before she threw herself off the cliff.

I knew what had happened to Sarah, and what must soon happen to me.

I had guessed before, and doubted my sanity, and denied my terror. I could deny it no longer.

Jeremy was a vampire, sustaining himself on living creatures. A vampire with a depraved hunger for living blood.

And now, when he reproached me for moving, for spoiling the pose, his deep soft voice was full of satisfaction, of need assuaged and appeased.

I summoned meager strength, forcing an apology, managing a faint smile. For my life's sake, I had to pretend, to hide revulsion boundlessly deep, and an all-enveloping mindless fear. I said, "I'm sorry, Jeremy. I'm just so tired now. Would you be angry if we stop for today?"

"You're always so tired lately," he complained.

I wondered if he was mocking me. But he was right. For weeks now I'd known of my waning strength and wondered at it. For weeks I'd sensed a slow change in me.

124

Dr. Benson had told me that I was anemic, as if I'd lost a lot of blood. Now I understood.

I rose slowly, carefully, and Jeremy came and encircled me with his arm, saying that he would take me to my room.

"I'm all right," I said quickly, and shrank at his touch.

He gave me a look, and that time I knew for sure that he was mocking me, enjoying a play on words that could be taken two ways, though I was supposed to know only one of them. He said, "Why, Teena, dear, how can you be so shy with me? After all, we *are* engaged. You mustn't act as if I'm a monster when I touch you."

He led me down the hall to my room, still holding me, and smiled at me, and told me to rest.

I wondered how I would find the courage, and the strength, to face the ordeal that lay ahead of me.

I spent the rest of the day in my room, the door carefully locked.

Estrella came and tried to talk to me, and complained that she still hadn't been able to reach Rory, and went away again.

Jeremy spent half an hour teasing me to come out, and finally gave up.

At dusk, when I knew Mrs. Foxall would be leaving, I made my way downstairs.

I was just in time to intercept her. "Were there any calls for me today?" I asked her.

She shook her head, peered into my eyes, then started out. I followed along with her, hurrying as she limped quickly down the driveway, as always making a wide circle away from the maze.

"You hate it, don't you?" I said, knowing she would understand.

She jerked her head once. "A bad place."

"Because of May?"

Mrs. Foxall reached for the gate. "Come with me, Teena. Now."

I might have said that I would. I might have gone with her then, and left Rentlow Retreat behind me for good, and never known the truth.

But Mrs. Foxall tugged the gate again, and frowned, and said, "What's wrong here?"

And Jeremy called from the terrace, "Is it still locked? Did you forget the release?"

Mrs. Foxall and I both turned back to him.

"Where are you going, Teena?" he called, smiling.

I said quickly, "Will you tell Rory? Please," and started for the terrace.

Jeremy went inside, and moments later, Mrs. Foxall had gotten the gate open and slipped through it and driven quickly away with her husband.

I prayed that she'd give Rory my message right away, that she'd understand why the gate had been locked and remained that way until I walked away from it, that she knew, as I did, that I was a prisoner in Rentlow Retreat.

Jeremy was back at the door to greet me when I reached the house.

His dark eyes glittered. "Feeling better now that you've rested all day?"

I nodded, though I was aware that I had had hardly strength enough to walk back to the terrace.

I knew that it meant I didn't have much time left. Not for what I had to do.

Aunt June and Estrella served the dinner that Mrs. Foxall had left.

I had offered my help, as usual, but Aunt June gave me a washed-out blue look and said, "Never mind, Teena. You seem somewhat tired this evening." She touched her forehead. "I just don't see how, when just yesterday, Dr. Benson said it was just my nerves . . ."

Uncle Charles glowered her into sudden silence, and she finished bringing the dishes in, then took her chair.

Estrella joined us, saying sullenly, "I don't know what's the matter with Rory! But I tell you . . ."

"What makes you think something is the matter?" Uncle Charles demanded.

"He's not been over, nor called. And that's not like him, and . . ."

"He has a few interests," Uncle Charles said coldly "beyond the Rentlows, I should hope."

A flush touched Estrella's cheeks. Her dark eyes slid toward me, but she didn't say anything.

It was an evening like all the others since I had arrived there.

I kept myself from dwelling on the awful secret I knew, lest my manner, or a chance word, give me away.

The others seemed quite the same to me.

And then Jeremy said, "I have the feeling that Teena's growing quite restive. We must do much more to amuse her, or else I suspect that we're going to wake up one morning and find she's gone."

I said quickly, "You've all been very good to me. Why say that, Jeremy?"

His eyes seemed to flare with hot lights, and his lips curled in a mocking smile. "Just a feeling, Teena love. Just as I have a feeling that you've decided you don't want to model any longer for me." He spread his smile around the table. "Isn't that a shame? Wouldn't it be a pity to have Teena's figure undone?"

"Oh, no," Estrella cried, giving me a quick anxious look. "What's the matter, Teena? Has Jeremy been working you too hard? You mustn't be angry with him. He just gets carried away. I'm sure that if you make the sessions shorter . . ."

"And if Teena won't," Jeremy asked humorously, "then who will?"

Uncle Charles' rimless glasses glittered at me.

Aunt June gave me an anguished look, then stared down at the food she hadn't touched.

I said carefully, "I don't know what Jeremy's talking about. We worked for hours today."

"Yes, we did, didn't we?" His voice was silky. "And will we do the same tomorrow?"

I tried to make myself sound indifferent, casual. "If you want to."

"Thank you, Teena," he said gently, and went on, "and as for our wedding plans . . ."

"I've explained, Jeremy."

He gave Uncle Charles a humorous look. "Six months, she says. Can you imagine? Until Margaretha returns from

127

her honeymoon, and"—he glanced at me—"and until her father can be here to give her away."

Uncle Charles deliberately put down his fork. His stolid, lined face was red. "It isn't seemly for a girl, a child really, to lay down conditions, Teena. We have had nothing to do with your family for many years. I do not plan to change that."

"I'm sorry." I met Uncle Charles' grim gaze. "I must have my family with me, or . . ."

"Or?" Jeremy asked softly.

"I'm sorry," I repeated, hurrying on. "Maybe we've made a mistake, Jeremy. Maybe you and I should take a little time to think things over."

"Teena!" Estrella seemed both terror-stricken and enraged at the same moment. "Teena Halliday, what's the matter with you?"

Uncle Charles said harshly, "I've always thought there was instability in the family." His gray eyes pointedly fixed on Aunt June.

She winced, turning her head away. "Charles, couldn't we . . ."

He went on, "Yes, that must be it. From the moment she came to this house, there's been nothing but one sign after another. I do think I shall have to do something about it." His threatening gaze touched me briefly, then moved to Jeremy. "Surely you agree?"

"Oh, she'll change her mind again," Jeremy said, smiling. "It's a woman's prerogative after all."

Uncle Charles' grim face didn't relax. He said, "It's the family arrogance all over again. Margaretha had it and showed it plainly. Yes, the way she left Ben Halliday for Arthur Haines proved it. Which is why we had nothing to do with her for so many years. She knew perfectly well that I disapproved, and didn't care. Not until she wanted to use us, to have Teena stay with us."

I thought it no wonder that Margaretha had spoken so rarely of the Rentlows if she'd known of Uncle Charles' dislike of her.

"And your father, Ben Halliday, had the same arrogance. Away he went, swearing she'd never hear from him again, not until he was a millionaire." Uncle Charles drew

128

a deep angry breath. "And he stuck to it too. That's arrogance for you."

I absorbed the meaning of Uncle Charles' words slowly. My father had sworn never to contact Mother or me until he was a millionaire. And Uncle Charles said that my father had stuck to his vow. But I had had a cable from my father. Which meant my father had become a millionaire. I kept my face blank, my eyes averted. But I asked myself silently how Uncle Charles knew what my father had done when they hadn't seen each other in twelve years. But they *had* seen each other—and recently. My father had been in Tumlee.

"And now you yourself, Teena," Uncle Charles went on balefully. "I hardly know what to think any more. We took you in when no one wanted you." He glared at Aunt June's whispered, "Oh, Charles, please . . ." "Then," he went on, "you lead Jeremy on to love you, now you . . ."

The gate signal in the pantry went off, a startling interruption.

No one moved.

I got to my feet, my heart beating hopefully.

"Please sit down," Uncle Charles told me. "We aren't expecting any one."

I sank into my chair.

"But it might be Rory," Estrella protested.

"We do not need company at the moment," Uncle Charles insisted.

Aunt June winced. "Charles, dear, you mustn't . . ."

He gave her a withering stare. "Do be quiet, June. I've had just about all the foolishness I intend to take from the members of your family. There will be no more."

The gate signal sounded again and again, until finally it went silent.

"If it was Rory, and I'll bet it was, then he's gone now," Estrella sighed.

"Yes," Uncle Charles said curtly. "We needn't fear our problems have to be aired before an audience." He went on, thoughtful and considering, "Arrogance and instability. It's been plain from the beginning. From the moment she arrived here. All that business about her

129

father. About Ben Halliday. A cable from him? Is that what she said? Then she must have sent it to herself. Why would Ben Halliday come here? Why would he say he'd meet her after twelve years? It was all some sad dream she's had. That's plain. You must remember that Margaretha is the same, June. Your sister. She's the cause of all of this. Remember that, June. She's the real cause."

It was on the tip of my tongue to defend myself, to tell Uncle Charles that I had proof that my father had been to Tumlee, to demand to know who Bethel Harper really was.

But I remembered Rory's warning. I sensed danger around me, though I couldn't define its source.

I managed to keep silent.

"We'll have to see what can be done about this," Charles said heavily.

I swallowed hard. I said softly, "I'm sorry you feel like this, Uncle Charles." I forced a brief, pained smile. "Believe me, I never intended to hurt you, nor Jeremy. But if a marriage won't do, surely it's best to find that out before and not after."

"Well said," Jeremy told me, "but I don't think you really know how you feel, Teena. We'll just wait and see, shall we?"

I nodded, went on quickly, "And as for what you said about my father. I'm sorry if my asking about him upset you. I didn't know there were hard feelings on your side. I did have the cable, but I realize it was either a prank, or else my father just changed his mind. I don't expect him to come here any more." I heard the tremor in my voice, stopped before I could give myself away completely by breaking into tears.

Yes, I had given up hope. Now that I was so sure Ben Halliday and Bethel Harper were the same man, I was sure that my father was dead.

Why? What had happened? I didn't know. But I was determined to find out.

And to do that I would have to survive. I would have to escape Jeremy's kisses.

I hoped that my calm, reasonable tone would per-

130

suade Uncle Charles and the others that I had no suspicions, no plans to try to leave.

I couldn't tell what any of them were thinking.

But Jeremy said, "We're all taking this much too seriously. As for you, Teena. I expect you'll change your mind about this too, and decide one of these days that you want more than anything else in the world to be Mrs. Jeremy Rentlow, and right away too, not after some six months."

"If it isn't because Rory has somehow turned her head," Estrella said spitefully.

My cheeks burned, but I said, "There's nothing between Rory and me, Estrella, and you know it."

Estrella shrugged as if she didn't believe me. I wondered why the truth wasn't evident to her.

Rory's interest in me was only based on his desire to know what had happened to Sarah. I was bait in a trap that he hoped to see sprung by Jeremy. Rory wanted to help me, but only because, through me, he thought he would learn the truth.

Painfully I acknowledged to myself what Estrella didn't believe. I winced, thinking of the safety I had once felt in Rory's arms, that I knew would never be mine again. I had relinquished any right to dream of that when I allowed Jeremy to charm me into an engagement I didn't want. I had no right to think of Rory as any more than an ally. Perhaps not even that.

Soon after, I rose, returned to my room. I sat down to outwait the slowly passing hours.

I knew what I had to do.

The moon rose high, casting a silver gleam over the green swoop of lawn that held the remains of Jeremy's animal victims, the cemetery where those beasts he had preyed upon were buried and marked by the statues he had done of them. Pale light touched the cold stone, and long slanting black shadows fell away from them.

The fountain that guarded the hedge maze whispered softly, and the world was black and still beyond the high stone wall and iron gate that guarded the place of death that was Rentlow Retreat.

I watched for a long time from the window. Then, my heart thudding with fear, I unlocked my door, stood still, listening.

Would Jeremy's door open, revealing his tall figure and bright mocking smile?

Would Estrella come out to demand where I was going?

Were Uncle Charles and Aunt June waiting for me?

The house was so still it seemed empty, so silent that I could hear the pounding of my blood in my ears.

I crept down the stairs, then out the door, and down the path towards the ridge.

I had to get to Rory.

For a moment, surrounded by whispery darkness, doubt touched me. He hadn't come, nor called. By now he had surely received the messages I had sent through Mrs. Foxall and Jimmie Hunnicut. Had Rory abandoned me?

I wouldn't allow myself to believe that. I scurried along the ridge, under Retreat Point, past the rhododendron bushes that hid the maze exit. Suddenly, just ahead, I saw the black night move and sway. Wide shoulders loomed large against the sky. Someone was waiting ahead, waiting for me on the shortcut to Rory's.

I hesitated for only an instant before I turned back the way I had come. Breath rasping in my throat, tear-blinded, and frightened, I crept into the house. I tiptoed into the pantry, sought the gate release and finally found it. Then, still listening hard, peering into the dark, I hurried outside.

I expected Jeremy to materialize from the shadows, to reach for me, smiling, to hold out his arms to encircle me.

I expected Uncle Charles to grab me, drag me back. But there was no movement, no sound.

I crossed the terrace and slipped down the driveway. I scurried past the green slope where the statues stood motionless in the moonlight, and past the white fountain at the entrance to the maze.

The tall iron gates loomed up ahead of me. I reached out to open them. But they held fast. I pulled and tugged and struggled with them, but they didn't give.

I knew that someone had followed me into the pantry, gone to the gate control. Someone had made sure that I couldn't escape.

CHAPTER FOURTEEN

Swift drowning terror held me, my fingers frozen to the gates, my pulse drumming in painful thunder at my temples.

And then, from the darkness around me, soft as the whisper of suddenly stirring leaves, I heard the soft hoarse call. "Teena? Teena? This way, Teena?"

The voice was faintly familiar.

Its impact was immediate.

Rory.

I threw a single glance toward the house, and saw in the moonlit grove a thick shadow move between the gleaming statues.

"Teena?"

"Oh, Rory, yes," I gasped. "I'm coming."

He had gotten my messages. He was here, waiting for me.

I plunged past the white fountain that sank softly, between the high black walls of the hedge maze, and into the direction from which his voice seemed to have come. A single glance behind me toward the grove proved that the thick shadow was drifting closer. I ducked deeper into the maze.

"Rory?" I whispered. "Where are you? Where? Someone's out there, Rory. Someone's coming."

There was movement behind me, a sound.

"Rory?"

Again movement, but closer.

"Answer me, Rory," I cried. "Answer me."

There was only silence. I saw the sudden glimmer of pale moonlight on an upraised arm. I saw a shadow wreathing a tilted back head. May Argon stood frozen before me.

Then I heard a sound, a sound too near. I turned and fled.

Whoever moved so carefully behind me was not Rory. That much I knew. He would have answered my call. He would have spoken.

133

Whoever had whispered my name, so familiar in the dark, had tricked me. It was a ploy that had been used before, I knew. I had heard my name said softly, gently, beneath my window the first night I'd come to Rentlow Retreat. Whoever had called me then had called me now. And now he stalked me, silent, watchful, waiting, through the maze.

The hedges were high black walls surrounding me. Walls that seemed to flicker with glints of light, tiny reflections of the splintered moon. The lane narrowed and widened under reaching branches, and at each crossing the statues stood silent and silvered, but peculiarly mobile, with long cold arms thrusting at me from the dark.

I fled, stumbling on the graveled lane, spinning from one turn to another, and found myself at a blank dead end. I crept back, retreating, and took a second turn. I tripped over a marble bench, bruising my knees and elbows, and rose to run again.

Behind me, stealthily, a figure that I couldn't see, that I didn't dare name, stalked me, hunted me down as if I were an animal being tracked to its death. I heard the whisper of footsteps, measured and calm, and infinitely terrifying. I heard the faint whisper of breath drawing closer, and the fainter whisper of leaves lightly touched as someone passed.

Breathless, exhausted, my will failing, I had to stop for an instant. And in that instant, the footsteps drew closer, and then paused too. Somewhere close by, someone else had stopped, stopped to breathe, to listen.

Was it Rory?

Jeremy?

Uncle Charles?

Could Aunt June be stalking me?

Or even Estrella?

I didn't know. I just didn't know, and I knew I must not wait to see.

When I went on, it was more slowly, quietly. I was too close to the limits of my strength to waste effort in running. Dr. Benson had said I was underweight and anemic. But I knew where my strength had gone, and how. I knew why Jeremy drew me into the white-walled studio, and

134

whispered sweet murmurings at me. And I knew that I would never be permitted to leave Rentlow Retreat. Not if the hunter who followed me could stop me.

So I went on slowly, carefully. I tried to remember the turns I had made, the direction I had taken, but I realized soon that I was hopelessly lost.

The maze of tall dark hedges was an enclosed world, peopled by dead and cold stone. I was trapped in it forever.

But I dared not stop again. The footsteps behind me seemed to draw closer and closer.

Hopelessly I stumbled on and on, taking the turns as they came, backing from blank emptiness to round a different corner, until suddenly from somewhere close by, I heard a soft laugh, a cold and soft laugh, and then Uncle Charles said, "Yes, Teena, you're doing nicely. Just keep going, and it will soon be at an end."

I froze, ducked close to the hedge wall.

He laughed softly again. "It's no use, Teena. You might as well go on."

I waited, breath held, not answering.

"Give up," he said. "You'll never escape me. Never. Never. You signed your death warrant at dinner tonight, and signed it again when you went to the gates tonight. First you made it plain that you refused to marry Jeremy, although you didn't quite put it that way. Then you made it plain that you guessed the truth and knew that you had to run away. Poor Teena, don't you know? You have no chance at all."

A cold chill threw a paralyzing net around me. I was motionless, bound. I waited, still listening.

Footsteps thudded in gravel. A shadow rose up.

I broke the web that held me and ran once again.

Behind me Uncle Charles came. "You can't escape me, Teena, no more than your father could. I can't see you, but I know you're there. It was the same that night. The night that your father died."

The pause was sudden, a listening pause.

I froze, held my breath. Uncle Charles had been trying to get me to give myself away, to answer him, cry out a protest.

I moved on as quietly as I could. But I was tear-blinded, trembling. My fears were no longer suspicions. Bethel Harper had been Ben Halliday. And he was dead. I would never see him now. The promises I had made myself for twelve years couldn't be kept.

"I wasn't good enough for your mother," Uncle Charles said in a low bitter whisper. "Not good enough for the beautiful Margaretha. Just as Jeremy is not good enough for the beautiful Teena, I suppose." There was a peculiarly grating chuckle. "So dear Margaretha turned me down and married Ben Halliday. It was a cruel blow to me. With all my hopes for Rentlow Retreat. But there was still June, so I married her. And then, then I discovered how they had both tricked me. A fine house and fine clothes, but none of it theirs. Creditors standing three deep at the door they couldn't call their own. I swore I'd get even. Ben Halliday laughed. He stopped laughing when Margaretha left him for Arthur Haines and Arthur Haines' money. Ben didn't laugh after that. Not until he found Alaskan oil."

Slowly, stealthily, listening but not daring to make a sound, I went on.

The voice trailed me. "Teena? Are you listening to me? You're an oil heiress. Doesn't that please you? Doesn't that thrill you? Won't your mother be destroyed when she discovers what she's lost? And I've gained?"

Ben was dead, and I was his heir. I began now to understand.

But Uncle Charles' whispery voice went on. "He came here, laughing again, gay, on top of the world. He came here and told me about his will. He would leave everything to you, he said. Everything, Teena. All that black gold pouring out of Alaskan soil would be yours. And in that same week Margaretha's letter arrived. Your Aunt June told him that you'd be coming. He laughed harder and longer, and said he couldn't wait. I suppose that was when he cabled you."

I forced one foot after another, dogged, determined, yet hopeless.

Uncle Charles was close behind me now. "We walked that night. We walked together. We came through the

136

maze, with me just behind him, as I'm behind you now, Teena. And somehow, somehow, we ended up at Retreat Point, and poor Ben Halliday fell to the rocks below."

The soft chuckle needed no underscoring. It was explanation enough.

I saw my father poised on the dread rock, and I saw him flung from it.

I knew Uncle Charles planned the same for me.

"He had to die," Uncle Charles was saying in a soft, reasonable whisper. "And it had to be before he saw you, told you. And once he was dead, I was his only living blood kin, Teena. I was his heir. Except for you. We buried Ben Halliday as Bethel Harper, and that left only you to deal with. Only you, poor Teena. How your Aunt June fought me! How poor little Estrella wept! Pleading with me to think of another way. To refuse to have you come. But there was only one way. And that was my way. You had to come. You had to die here. Then, in a little while, I would hear that Ben Halliday had died in Alaska. I would file his will, and as his only living heir, I would have for myself all his Alaskan oil gold."

I made a turn, then another. There was a tiny suggestion of an opening in the hedge walls. I thought I saw stars. I moved on hopelessly, certain now that Uncle Charles led me on by coming on behind me. Certain that he drove me on, knowing each step of the way, to the place where I would die.

"We managed to get Bethel Harper buried just in time, and then you were there, asking about your father. It was a shock, I can tell you." The soft terrible chuckle came again. "But I was up to it. We all were. Estrella and your aunt knew they had to be. For Jeremy's sake. Oh, yes, they've protected him since they've known and refused to know. And I made sure that they'd protect him, and me along with him, once again. I fixed the window frame, and called you in the night, but you saved yourself. I booby-trapped the mirror, and Rory was there to pull you away from its crushing weight. And then I saw what Jeremy wanted of you. It would have been perfect, perfect. You'd have married him, and been Ben

Halliday's heir. But only for a little while. How long could you have lasted as Jeremy's bride? And then he would have owned Ben Halliday's Alaskan oil. But no, Teena, no. You refused. You knew Jeremy for what he was, didn't you? And you suspected the truth about Bethel Harper. And you determined to work your will against mine. Poor Teena. Didn't you know that you'd never escape Jeremy? And if you did, then you'd have me to contend with!"

The tiny opening in the hedge wall loomed larger. The suggestion of stars had become real, bright. There was moon-streaked sky, and below it a narrow ridge of black.

I stepped cautiously from between the dark walls that had imprisoned me into the thick rhododendron bushes.

I fought my way through to freedom, air, and saw just above me the harsh jutting outline of Retreat Point.

There was thrashing behind me, and soft chuckling laughter, and the shadows broke into reaching arms. I flung myself sideways, but a thick weight buried me, rolled me, thrust me. I lay half on rock, half in air, my eyes widening at the sight of silvered whitecaps below, and the dark jagged teeth of boulders reaching up for me.

"Like your father," Uncle Charles panted. "Unstable. The whole family. And I'll have it all, Teena. As I should. Since it's mine."

He dragged me to my knees. I felt the wind touch my hair, and death touch my cheeks.

I looked into a face terrible to see, a face unmasked, and twisted with hate and the hope of murder.

And then, from the dark beyond his shoulder, a shadow shifted and drew closer. It became tall and rugged against the sky. Soundlessly, touched by moonlight, an auburn head nodded at me.

I flung myself down, dragging Uncle Charles with me. I kicked and bit and clawed, while he cursed me, struggling to hold me and throw me over the edge of Retreat Point.

What must only have been an instant's terror seemed to linger for hours. Weakening, shivering, fighting still, I

138

was suddenly free, sprawling in the brush below the ridge.

Above me, at the brink of Retreat Point, I saw Uncle Charles locked in desperate struggle with a tall, auburn-touched shadow. I saw Uncle Charles break loose, and step back, and hang briefly in empty air before he disappeared.

The tall slim shadow cast a single glance downward, then jumped from the ridge and drew me to my feet. Arms closed around me. A heart pounded against mine.

"It's all over," Rory said. "Close, God forgive me, but all over, Teena."

I shivered against him. Uncle Charles was gone. He could no longer harm me. But what of Jeremy? Jeremy?

"It's all over," Rory repeated, his arms tightening, as he lifted his head.

I knew without looking. I knew by my own breathlessness. I knew by my terror.

Rory was looking at Jeremy.

He stood in the moonlight at the foot of Retreat Point, faintly smiling. "How long have you known?" he asked Rory. "When did you guess?"

"A long time ago," Rory answered. "Back when May Argon died. But I didn't believe it. I couldn't believe it, Jeremy."

"Who would?" Jeremy asked. "And of course it was Sarah . . ."

"Yes," Rory agreed. "It was Sarah's death that forced me to accept it. And as soon as I saw Teena I knew it would happen again."

"What a pity," Jeremy answered. "They were all always so good to me, you know. I'd liked to have done something for them. For Charles, and June, and Estrella. They loved me so much. They loved me too much to betray me." He laughed softly. "But of course they'd never sit for me. Not that I ever wanted them to. Except maybe for Estrella. I love beauty, you know. A pure line, a smooth throat, a sleek wing. Beauty." Again he laughed softly. "Beauty, Teena."

I trembled, and Rory's arms were warm and strong, tightening around me.

139

Jeremy glanced toward Retreat Point. "He's gone, isn't he?"

Rory nodded.

Jeremy raised his hand in a salute, smiled briefly, and turned away. He took a long step down, then another.

"Jeremy, wait," Rory said.

"Nothing will happen to me," Jeremy said, his voice fading as he moved further away. "I'm going to find his body."

Moments later, watching from the ridge, Rory and I saw Jeremy. He stood on the jagged rocks below, no more than a single small shadow, shifting back and forth in obvious search.

The white whirling waves washed over the boulders and drew away in spinning cesspools. One of them rose up to Jeremy's thighs, and when it receded, he went with it, slowly and steadily disappearing into the dark.

When he was quite gone, I whispered, "Now it's over, Rory. Only now."

He nodded and drew me with him toward the house.

On the way he told me that he had spent most of the day on the telephone, checking my father's whereabouts, and past life, and discovered, as Uncle Charles had told me, that my father had become a millionaire, and that he had last been seen in Tumlee, and that the authorities agreed that he had probably been buried as Bethel Harper and would soon know for certain. Rory had received the messages I had sent him through Mrs. Foxall and Jimmie, and had come to Rentlow Retreat at dinnertime, hoping to see me and take me away. "I knew I had to by then," Rory said. "Mr. Jessup said there'd been letters for you, though not for your father. And Mrs. Foxall said Jeremy didn't let her go through the gate until he saw you start back for the house. So I realized Jeremy and Charles guessed you were suspicious of them, and that maybe I was too. That," Rory explained, his green eyes narrowed with remembered pain, "was just what I was afraid of all along. From the moment I saw you, I knew Jeremy would want you. Then you started asking me about your father. I was afraid to warn you against Jeremy, to let you know the gossip

140

in Tumlee, lest you inadvertently give something away. But I watched you, pretending as I had ever since Sarah's death, to be interested in Estrella, and I saw what was happening to you, and when I got Dr. Benson to check you, he agreed that you were falling ill, just as Sarah had, though he didn't accept my explanation for it at all, I must say."

I shuddered. "If Jeremy hadn't wanted me, then Charles would have managed somehow for me to die."

"In a fall from Retreat Point," Rory agreed. "Like May Argon. Who may or may not have jumped. Jeremy was just about fifteen then. May was his first figure. Mrs. Foxall told me how wildly May talked for a while just before her death. It was just after Sarah died that Mrs. Foxall came to me with her ideas about it, and decided then to go to work for the Rentlows. They tried to control him, you know. He never left the grounds, except for a very occasional trip to Tumlee, and they had no one here, not until your father came, and then you. So . . ." Rory's voice went bitter. "So there was the animal cemetery instead. And Rentlow Retreat became death-cursed."

As we crossed the terrace, the door opened slowly.

Estrella stood there, her dark eyes wide and blank.

Aunt June was with her.

I stopped, clung to Rory. "I can't go in there," I said in a whisper. "Rory, I just can't."

"No," he agreed. "Never again."

"He was such a good boy," Aunt June told us softly. "Always, always so good, so loving. And then, when he was fifteen . . ." Her voice broke. She sobbed, "How could it have happened to a sweet boy like Jeremy? What devil possessed him?"

No one answered her. No one knew what to say.

She went on. "I didn't want it to happen, Teena. I tried to protect you. When you first came, and Charles—well, you must know. And then Jeremy . . . but Charles promised it wouldn't be like before. If you married him, you'd be safe. That's what Charles said. And suddenly I saw how you were fading. I was so afraid, so terribly afraid . . ."

141

"We were all afraid," Estrella said harshly. "But it's over now. We'll never have to be afraid again." She stepped back, drawing Aunt June with her, and the door closed softly.

Rory led me across the terrace, down the driveway past the moon-silvered slope where Scuffy stood, past the white fountain that marked the hedge maze, to the high iron gates.

He touched them, and I held my breath until they slowly swung open. We walked through them together, and they silently closed behind us.

I paused in the lane. I didn't know where I would go next, or what would happen, but I already knew that saying goodbye to Rory would be greater anguish than I could bear.

I remembered doubting him, with shame.

I remembered trusting him, with longing.

He said, "I watched the house from the shortcut, Teena. I was so sure you'd come that way, come to me. I was waiting there, and I actually saw you, and then you turned and ran back to the house. I cut around the outside, trying to head you off, but you got past me in the dark. The next thing I knew, you were at the gate. And I saw Charles creeping toward you, though I wasn't sure then that it was he."

"He called to me. I thought it was you. For just a minute I thought it was you because it had a familiar sound to it. But he had called me that way before, and as soon as I was in the maze, I realized it, and I knew I was lost."

"I saw you disappear inside. It was obvious what he planned. I raced around to the exit to wait for you there."

"I didn't know that, Rory. All that time, running ahead of him, I thought I was completely alone."

He smiled down at me. "You'll never again be alone, Teena." I leaned against him joyfully, knowing that I wouldn't have to face the anguish of saying goodbye after all.